the in-between

st. martin's griffin ≈ new york

the in-between

barbara stewart

This is a work of fiction. All of the characters, organizations, and events portrayed in this novel are either products of the author's imagination or are used fictitiously.

www.stmartins.com

Design by Anna Gorovoy

Library of Congress Cataloging-in-Publication Data

Stewart, Barbara, 1970–
    The in-between / Barbara Stewart. — 1st. Ed.
        p. cm.
ISBN 978-1-250-03016-0 (trade paperback)
ISBN 978-1-250-03017-7 (e-book)
1. Supernatural—Fiction.   2. Best friends—Fiction.   3. Friendship—
Fiction.   4. Near-death experiences—Fiction.   5. Grief—Fiction.
6. Single-parent families—Fiction.   7. Moving, Household—
Fiction.   I. Title.
PZ7.S84873In 2013
[Fic]—dc23
                                                        2013025064

First Edition: November 2013

10   9   8   7   6   5   4   3   2   1

for dave

acknowledgments

I owe a world of thanks to the following: My husband, Dave, for always believing in me. My mom and dad, for never discouraging any dream, no matter how crazy. My late grandmother, for letting me stay up until the wee hours watching scary movies with her. Kelly, for being an awesome sister and for raising three remarkable children—Mary, Sarah, and Fred—who constantly amaze me with their intelligence, humor, and compassion. My agent, Amy Tipton, and my editor, Vicki Lame, for their enthusiasm and hard work making this book a reality. For teaching me how to write a good story: Naton Leslie and Richard Spilman. For being kind readers and stellar in-laws: Fred, Bob, and Sue. Thank you.

part i

from the lost journal
of elanor moss

*Hope is the thing with feathers
that perches in the soul.*
—Emily Dickinson

one

I was pronounced dead at the scene of the accident. My lifeless body slumps over the cat carrier in the backseat of the twisted wreck. Bloodstains bloom through my T-shirt and jeans, and my hair sparkles with bits of broken glass. My parents sparkle and bloom, too. They are in the front seat, pinned upright by the dashboard of our crappy little hatchback. The airbags slowly deflate, floating down over them like freshly washed sheets. My mother's cheek is pressed against the side window. My father's head droops, his chin on his chest. Even with all the blood we look peaceful, as if we're napping at a rest stop before continuing the long drive to our new home.

Were my earbuds still in my ears when the rescue team arrived? Was Lucy making that strangled calling noise she makes when she can't find me? Did they use one of those metal saws to free us? All I know is some stubborn paramedic refused to give up on me. Maybe because I'm only fourteen. Maybe because he has a daughter or little sister who listens to the same music and has an orange-and-white cat or wears all black and loves cheese-filled pretzels.

I am alive. My father, too. My mother is gone. Lucy is gone. That's what I know. Here's what I don't know: Where did my mother die? (The middle of the highway? The back of an ambulance? On a stainless steel gurney in a fluorescent-lit ER?) Where is she buried? Did Lucy die or is she lost? (Lost seems worse.) How long was I in the hospital? (Long enough to lose most of the fifteen pounds I'd put on during The Worst Year of My Life. Long enough for my hair to grow out. Long enough for the red scars on my wrists to fade to white.)

Here is what I remember before everything changed forever: We were somewhere in the mountains of Pennsylvania—the Poconos, I think. My dad was driving. My mother was in the passenger seat warning me not to let Lucy out of the cat carrier again.

"She's miserable," I said.

"She's a cat," my mother said. "She'll survive."

My father smiled in the rearview mirror. "Watch it or we'll put you in a carrier."

I poked a cheese-filled pretzel through the metal gate. Lucy loves salt but she ignored it. I popped it in my mouth and chewed.

"That's enough," my mother said, reaching behind her. "Give me the bag."

I plugged in my earbuds and ate one more. New Ellie is addicted to cheese-filled pretzels, too.

"Richard? Talk to your daughter, please. We had an agreement. She's going to start eating better. No more junk food."

We were starting over. This was our New Beginning. Not just for me, but for all of us. A few weeks after his unemployment ran out, my father was offered a job in a water treatment lab in Potts-ville, New York. My mother was going to get her real estate li-cense. I was going to lose weight and dress better and not try to kill myself again.

Honestly, right then, things were good. Better than they'd been in a long time. It's surprising what distance can do. I was obsessed with the number of miles between me and Jackson Mid-dle and everyone in it, especially Priscilla Hodges. I asked my dad for an odometer reading.

"Three-ninety-one, kiddo." He winked. "Nope . . . wait . . . make that three-ninety-two."

We were driving into a bank of clouds parked low over the mountain, but the darkness was lifting. My heart was lifting. I felt lighter than sunshine. I wanted to live forever.

Before I tried to end it all, Old Ellie's favorite morbid pastime had been imagining her own death: school shooting, E. coli, ter-rorist attack. It's what got her through the endless days at Jack-son Middle. God, how they shunned me. Correction: shunned *her*. Old Ellie had low self-esteem. Old Ellie had dependent per-sonality disorder. Old Ellie engaged in self-destructive thought. But Old Ellie always had Scilla. It was the two of us against the world until . . .

Stop. Just stop. I know what happened. I've got a box of jour-nals documenting your stupid, sorry life. This is not about Old Ellie. This is not about Priscilla. This is about New Ellie and Mom and Dad and Lucy.

"Can you turn down the air? I'm cold."

Those were my last words before I died. Poignant, right? For someone who loves books and spent hours planning her own an-nihilation, you'd think I could have come up with something a little more poetic. At least I get a do-over.

Mom's last words: "Oh my God!"

And now I'm here. We're here. Without Mom. I woke this morning with my father staring down at me, a look of joy (or was it horror?) distorting his face.

"Where are we?" I said.

I was in my bed, but not in my room. I sat up and looked around, and then it hit me: the new house. We'd made it. It was all a bad dream. New Ellie was in her new room. It was nicer than I remembered from our trip back in June when we'd flown to Pottsville to go house hunting. My father had painted it the colors I'd picked: Nacho Cheese and Chips.

"Where's Mom?"

I tried to get up.

"You shouldn't even be here," my father whispered, tucking my comforter around me. "Stay in bed. You need to rest."

"What happened?"

"You don't remember?"

I remembered my dream: I remembered asking Mom to turn down the air. I remembered her reaching for the knob on the dashboard and gazing up through the windshield at the southbound lane. I remembered the way the headlights looked like Christmas lights strung across the mountain above us.

"Oh my God!" My mother clapped her hand over her mouth and pointed.

A black-and-silver RV had gone through the guardrail. It was airborne, nose-diving down the mountain towards us. My father punched the gas. My head snapped back. The RV somersaulted, and pieces of metal and plastic rained down. I grabbed the cat carrier and closed my eyes. I remembered the brakes squealing. I remembered the seat belt locking, digging into my chest. I remembered my pulse rushing in my ears, and my father yelling, "Hold on! We're gonna hit—"

"We crashed," I said.

My father nodded. "You were hurt pretty bad."

I felt fine. No cuts or bruises or broken bones. I wiggled my fingers and toes.

"You hit your head."

I felt for bandages.

"Inside." My father drummed his temple. "Let me know if you feel dizzy."

My father made me poke-in-the-eye eggs and bacon, then dragged a chair beside my bed and watched me eat. He had this hopeful, tender look, like he was caring for an injured bird.

I chewed my food and smiled at Dad and gave the eggs a thumbs-up. They were good, but not as good as Mom's. Then I realized what I already knew—in my heart. My mother was gone. She hadn't made it. My father didn't have to say it. It was written in the lines across his forehead, in those sad watery eyes of his. Everything went blurry. I tried swallowing, but there was a knot in my chest. My throat tightened around a clot of warm yolk.

I put down the fork and closed my eyes, trying to breathe. Everything I'd suffered over the last year was nothing compared to this. I'd hated my mother that day in the family therapist's office when she turned to me and said, "You don't know grief. You don't know misery."

But she'd been right.

My father squeezed my hand. I opened my eyes to look at him. But his palms—both palms—were pressed into his eye sockets, like he was trying to keep from seeing something terrible.

I felt it again. A clutching. Invisible fingers kneading. Warm. Soft. Something brushed my face. My skin tingled. Not my father, but just as familiar. It felt like . . . it felt like her.

"Do you think Mommy's still with us?" I asked.

My father wiped his eyes. "What?"

I felt it again. A grip so tight it made my bones ache.

"I think my brain's messed up."

"You're in shock," my father said, reaching for the curled hand at my side.

I pulled away. I didn't want the feeling to pass. But it did. Just like that, whatever it was let go.

My father carried the tray of dishes downstairs and didn't come back. I heard the strains of some sad jazz saxophone echoing through the house. I don't know what he was doing down there. Probably the same thing as me—trying to get settled. God, there's so much to do. Everything I own is in boxes, tubs, and bags. I made sure the movers hadn't damaged the important stuff—my Pegasus collection, the dollhouse my mother built—before I ran out of steam. I felt weak and achy, like I was coming down with something. I sat at the desk and switched on the lamp. It was getting dark. Correction: darker. It had been gray and murky all afternoon. The kind of day that makes you think all the color has been drained out of the world.

It's night now. Nine, maybe. I can't find my alarm clock or even a calendar. And it's damp and chilly, the kind of night Mom would've fixed soup for dinner or called for pizza. It feels more like October than . . .

I breathe in sharply.

It's happening again. I feel her.

This isn't my brain short-circuiting or shock. It's as if my hand has a life of its own, the fingers uncurling one by one.

Scilla and I used to play this game called knife. I would make a fist (tight, tighter), and she would caress my knuckles, my wrist, the back of my hand. (Concentrate. Concentrate. People dying, babies crying. Concentrate. Concentrate.)

"Close your eyes," she'd whisper, peeling back my fingers, exposing my palm. (Babies dying, people crying. Concentrate. Concentrate.)

No matter how many times we'd done it, it was always a shock when she stabbed me with her thumbnail. (Stick a knife in your hand, let the blood run down. Stick a knife in your hand, let the blood run down.) Just thinking about her fingers tickling across my wrist and down my arm gives me chills. I swear I used to feel the blood pooling in the crook of my arm.

Does Scilla know my mother is dead?

Something soft presses against my forehead. A rush of breath warms my skin. She's here. My mother's here. I know it.

two

When we were in fifth grade, Scilla's dad got his arm chewed off in a machine at work. He used to tell us about his ghost pains. It's a condition amputees feel after losing a limb. He used to show us his stump, all pink and shiny, like something boiled. He said he could still feel sensations like heat and pressure and tingling, but it wasn't real. He said the brain can't accept such a sudden, shocking loss. It keeps firing impulses to the nerves that used to be connected to the missing part. Maybe that's all this is, what I'm feeling with my mom: a physical memory. My brain's screwed-up response to losing her. My body's way of consoling my grief-stricken mind.

three

I left the second floor this morning and took a tour of the house. It's okay. No one will mistake us for millionaires. It's small and old and creaky and backs up to the woods. My parents called it a "fixer-upper." It would look a thousand times better if my father would unpack.

It's quiet without Mom. She would have been better at dealing. Dad and I are stuck, useless. Mom could handle anything. When I tried to kill myself, she was the one who kept everything going. It's how she coped, by doing things. Every day she'd force me out of bed and out of sweats and make me shower and wash what little I had left of my hair. My dad is the one who went to pieces. He couldn't even talk to me. He'd just stand in my doorway, staring at me like I was a stranger in his daughter's bed.

Mom was the enthusiastic one, the confident one, the glass-is-half-full one. My father gets depressed. He goes off the rails. He loses hope. They were a good match. Opposites attract and all that. My mother used to say I'm just like my father. Maybe, but I've got her in me, too. I can feel it sometimes—her optimism—deep inside, struggling to surface.

I'm not saying my mother was perfect, but everything would've been running smoothly by now—the curtains hung, the dishes unpacked, the TV hooked up. I'm going through withdrawal. There's no TV because there's no cable. No cable equals no Internet. No Internet equals no e-mail.

We're living like hoarders. The house is a maze of boxes and trash bags. There's shredded paper all over the carpets. It looks like a parade went through the living room. I'd clean it up if I could find the vacuum. None of the furniture is arranged. Everything's still sitting wherever the movers happened to plunk it down. We don't even have a phone. We combed the house for the cell, but it's gone.

I don't know what my father does all day. We don't *do* anything. We haven't gone anywhere. He hasn't unpacked his telescope. He just shuffles from room to room, poking through junk, searching for something he never seems to find. Truthfully I don't know what I do all day, either. I'm missing enormous chunks of time. One minute I'm painting my nails or going through pictures of Mom, and then . . . I don't know, my brain checks out for an hour or two. It feels like hours, anyway. I have to go by the light. All the clocks are still packed. My father lost his watch in the accident. It was brand new. My mother had engraved it for their anniversary: *You make every minute worth remembering.* Corny, I know, but he loved it.

I am seriously damaged. The blackouts are one thing, but most of my senses are broken, too. I can still hear. And my sense of touch seems heightened—my left hand, especially, the hand the in-between 13

my mother always holds. It's the other senses that aren't working. I can't smell. I can't taste. Even my sense of color is off. Everything is dull and drab, like seeing the world through a dirty
window. My room is yellow, but it's definitely not Nacho
Cheese—it's the color of sickness, of infection. It's like that with
everything. Reds and pinks have a brownish tinge to them, the
look of dried blood. Blue doesn't even register—it all looks gray.
Which is depressing because I love color. You'd never know it by
the way I dress. My closet looks like a black hole. But that was supposed to change. That was part of the New Beginning. Mom was
going to take New Ellie on a back-to-school shopping spree for all
new clothes—colorful clothes, stylish clothes, clothes that fit.

On the bright side (if there's a bright side to any of this), my
fat jeans are too big. I had to dig around for something smaller.
It's been so long I've forgotten what it's like to wear clothes that
don't pinch. And my hair looks good, too. It's growing back thick
and dark and shiny. I don't know what possessed Old Ellie to
hack it all off that day. She just started cutting and couldn't stop.

What's happening to my father? He's not himself. He's like the
living dead. I've seen him depressed. That's nothing new. It happens every Christmas, and sometimes around his birthday. This
is something different. Worse than the time he and Mom almost
separated, or the time they were having money troubles and almost lost the house. Worse even than when I tried to die. It's
like all those other bouts of depression were just tremors, little
quakes. Losing Mom is too big. The world is crashing down and
all he can do is stand and watch, alone and terrified, powerless to
go on living.

I'm here, but I'm not Mom. I can't talk to him the way she
talked to him.

Don't get me wrong. He's not totally neglectful. He turns off my light at night and tucks me in. Yesterday he tried to help me find the blow dryer. Tonight he opened a can of soup and made grilled cheese for dinner. It's better than nothing, I guess, even if it was just soup and sandwiches. We were actually okay for a while, staring into our bowls, and waiting for the soup to cool. But then we had to ruin it by talking.

Dad: Aren't you gonna eat?

Me: I'm eating.

Dad: No, you're not. What's wrong with it? It says you can
use water. Is it better with milk?

Me: It's okay. My taste buds aren't working.

Dad: Maybe you're catching a cold.

Me: There's other stuff wrong, too. Weird stuff.

Dad: Like what?

Me: I feel like Mommy's been holding my hand.

I wasn't supposed to see it, the face he made before he tried to look curious. That split second when his eyeballs shifted toward the ceiling, showing too much white. That face that said, *C'mon, Ellie*. He didn't believe me.

What I said next was meant to hurt him, but it was also true. I didn't make it up. "No one's waiting for us on the other side. All those stories about near-death experiences? Heaven doesn't exist. There's no white light. Mommy wasn't there. When you die, you die. That's it."

My dad just sat there, spoon raised, blinking. He let out a rush of breath and pushed himself up and shuffled over and cradled my face in his hands.

"Ellie, sweetie, I don't know what to tell you," he said. "If you feel like she's with you—"

I lifted my chin and searched his eyes. Nothing. I didn't have to ask, but I did.

"You don't feel her?"

He shook his head. His face crumpled.

I feel New Ellie retreating. Old Ellie's slithering back. We're just barely living. We should've all died in the accident. We would've been better off.

four

the sky outside my window is clear and bright, but this house is shut up like a tomb. I want to go out, but I can't. I'm afraid of the blackouts. Plus, there's nowhere to go. Everywhere I look it's mountains and trees and more mountains. I didn't remember it being so desolate, so quiet. It's like living in the bottom of a bowl. Where we live is hardly a town, just a road with some houses and a river. Even the name sounds Podunk-y: Pottsville. What were my parents thinking? No stores. No gas stations. No restaurants. The library is five miles away in a bigger small town. The nearest mall? God only knows. It might as well be on the moon.

five

i can't get out of bed. My skin's clammy. My hair is flat and greasy. And my eyes are raw from crying. I just sleep and sleep and sleep. My father doesn't see anything wrong. He brings me juice and cereal and cheese-filled pretzels. He's not Mom. He doesn't whirl around my room like a cheery tornado. He knows what it's like. He feels my pain.

I miss Mom. I miss my Lucy Cat. I miss Priscilla. She ruined my life but I'd give anything to talk to her. She'd understand. She'd listen. She was my best friend. My Scilla Monster. She wouldn't have to tell Natalie Paquin. She wouldn't have to tell anyone at Jackson Middle.

It could be our secret.

six

i hate the saying "When one door closes, another door opens." My life has been nothing but doors shutting in my face. Doors do not open for Ellie. They only close . . . until today.

"Earth to Ellie. Hey, it's me."

I don't know how long she'd been standing there—A minute? A lifetime?—but I flung my pen like a spaz and stuffed the letter I'd been writing in the drawer. Shimmering in the doorway was the most beautiful human being I've ever seen. Dark hair. Bright blue eyes. Just like me, but the similarities end there. With a body like hers, she has to be an athlete. Probably a runner. I'm too chunky to wear clothes like hers: flouncy dress and fingerless gloves, feather earrings and killer silver boots. It was a weird combination, but she pulled it off without looking clowny or skanky. I would look like a clown. Priscilla would look like a skank.

"I didn't mean to scare you," she said and strolled over and scooped up the pen.

There was something about her that was familiar, but I knew we'd never met. I didn't think there was any way I would forget someone like her. I racked my damaged brain.

"You don't remember me. I know. You've been through a lot." She cocked her hip and tapped the pen against her teeth. "We'll fix that." She took my hand—my left hand, my mother's hand—and wrote her name on my palm, just like this:

MADELINE TORUS

All caps. Not like me, using all lowercase in my old journals. In English, too, until my teacher threatened to fail me. I stared at my palm. There was an instant connection I couldn't explain. Even her name was familiar. Like something remembered from a dream. Forgetting her would be like forgetting a part of who I am, like the scars on my wrists or my birthday.

I hadn't said a single word since she'd walked through the door. I looked into those big blue eyes and tried to speak, but my mouth went dry. Madeline tilted her head, waiting. My face grew hot as the seconds passed. I worried she could hear my heart thumping madly in my chest. Of course I couldn't say something normal, like "What's up?" or "Cool boots."

"I like your eyes," I whispered. "You have pretty eyes."

Dork. Loser. This is why I don't have any friends. Girls don't say things like that to each other. That's how rumors get started. I bit my lip and stared at my knees, waiting for her to say she had the wrong house, the wrong Ellie.

"You have pretty eyes, too," she said. She sounded like she

meant it, but I knew she didn't. I don't have pretty eyes. They're small and a little too close, and skitter back and forth when I'm nervous.

"I wouldn't lie to you," she said softly. She took my hand and led me to the middle of the room where we sat on my rug face-to-face, crisscross applesauce.

She knows me, this Madeline Torus. We've met. We've talked. I've told her things about myself.

"So, Elanor Moss . . . Ellie," she said. "You're fourteen. You love cheese-filled pretzels. You love Halloween more than Christmas. You hate the word 'pianist' 'cause it sounds dirty. You're into poetry and music and art that is dark and depressing and weird. You like things that make you think, make you feel something. But you like sweet stuff, too. Your favorite animal is the pygmy marmoset."

My face flushed hotly. I just knew any minute a bunch of people were going to jump out of the closet, laughing their heads off at my stupidity. It sounds crazy, I know. But Madeline Torus is not the kind of person who would be friends with someone like me.

"Are you okay?" she said. "I can stop. I don't have to talk about this if you don't want."

I played it cool. I didn't want her thinking I was a head case. And I didn't want her to stop. It was a first for me, having someone act like I'm interesting, like I'm something special. It's like my life is a television show she's been following since the first episode. I nodded for her to continue.

"You were in an accident. A really bad one. You lost your mother and maybe your cat. Lucy, right? You hurt your head and you're having blackouts. You're lonely right now because your best friend in the world—Priscilla Hodges—ditched you for a snob named Natalie Paquin."

What hadn't I told her? I was sweating through my sweats. The room was a furnace. I tried opening the window, but my father had painted it shut. I started searching through my dresser—I had something sharp somewhere—and caught a glimpse of myself in the mirror.

I'm not trying to be vain, but I'm not totally ugly. I have some good qualities—not many, but some. I have nice eyebrows and a smallish nose and okay skin. But then my focus shifted to Madeline coming up behind me, smiling at my reflection. All the makeup in the world couldn't make me that kind of pretty. I'm thinner than I was, but I'm still heavy. My body eclipsed hers, like the moon blotting out the sun. I hated it. The only thing we have in common besides our hair and our eyes is our height. I would've said she was taller, but she's not. With her head on my shoulder we looked like a two-headed freak. Madeline smiled secretively. I smiled, too, and it felt good. It felt good to smile at someone who smiled back.

"What do you want most in the world?" she asked.

To be loved, I thought. But I knew that would sound corny and needy and might make her leave forever—so I never really answered. Instead, I said, "Can I try your boots?"

She went over to the chair and took them off, chucking them across the room. I sat on the bed and pulled them on. They fit. Madeline tucked a strand of hair behind her ear and froze. "You were writing when I came in," she said, staring at my desk as if she could see the grimy sheet of paper—tearstained and rambling and full of exclamation marks—hidden in the drawer. The Scilla Letter. I'd been working on it all morning, but now I was sickened by what I had written—a pathetic plea for her to give me another chance. I don't know why, but I took it out and let Madeline read.

"Oh, Ellie." She sounded disappointed. Not with me. With a world where someone like me would have to beg someone like Priscilla to be her friend. "She didn't deserve you," she said, crushing the paper in her fist and tossing it where it belonged—in the trash. "It's time to let go." She held out her hands for the boots.

"Stay with me," I pleaded.

"I'm right here," she said, placing her hand on my heart.

Madeline Torus. I know she's real because she wrote her name on my palm. I can see it, right there in blue ink. Without that, I'd think it was all a dream. Madeline and Ellie. Our names sound perfect together. Maybe Priscilla didn't deserve me. But what did I do to deserve Madeline? I want her with me, always. That's what I want most in the world. I'm drawn to her in a way I can't explain. My mother clutches my hand and I'm little again, waiting at a busy crosswalk. She knows how I get: obsessive, dependent, clingy. She's saying: Slow down. Give your friend room to breathe. Don't smother her. People don't like to be smothered.

seven

I f I close my eyes I can see her, an afterimage, as if I've been staring at the sun. She's standing in my doorway, looking down at me like the stone angel in the cemetery where Scilla and I used to hang out. It was an old cemetery, with hills and ravines, full of pines and weeping willows. We'd sneak past the caretaker's cottage and run like crazy past the crypts and the soldiers' field until we got to the clearing where the new bodies were buried. Then we'd stop, giggling and out of breath, by the statues. My angel had downcast eyes and a long, straight nose and a thick rope of hair that coiled noose-like around her neck. She was marble, I think, and her bare feet were green with lichen, her face and drape streaked black from acid rain.

Today has been a fog, but I think I'm getting better. I'm still having blackouts, but colors are starting to look normal again. Better than normal—everything glows. I can taste again, too, and smell things. This morning my father burnt the toast.

I need to see her. I need to see Madeline Torus. I need to talk to her. It's killing me not knowing when she'll be back. What if she never comes back? Her name on my palm is smudged and fading. Without her, I'm fading.

I don't know anything about her. I don't even know how to reach her. What's her phone number? Where does she live? What's her e-mail address? I asked my dad, but he looked confused. These days that's normal for him. I told him he needs to snap out of it—we have to go on living—but he just gave me this wretched look like I was torturing him.

I want to be prepared for when she comes back. I have to live like she might show up any minute. I can't let myself crash and burn with my father. He's like that RV that plunged through the guardrail, torpedoing through space, destroying everything in its path. I have to steer clear. I have to get out of bed and shower and brush my teeth and wear long-sleeve shirts to cover my wrists. I have to keep my room clean.

After breakfast I scrubbed the bathroom. My father had gotten whiskers all over everything. (But at least he's still shaving.) I bleached the rust ring on the sink from his shaving cream can, put the toilet paper in the roll holder, and cleared a little spot on the vanity for my makeup. The only lights are two fluorescent tubes on either side of the medicine cabinet—one takes forever to come on, the other flickers and hums—but I don't know how to change them. It makes it hard to do your eyes, but I like it dark. I can't see my flaws. I wonder if that's how Madeline sees me? When I think of her I get this panicky rush, like I'm holding my breath. Probably because I am.

eight

hooked up the DVD player today. All our movies are dumb family classics or cheesy comedies, but the sound keeps me company. It's better than listening to my father bump around the house like a ghost. It's better than sitting in my room waiting for my stone angel to appear.

nine

"God, this place is depressing!"

That's what Madeline said when she sauntered into my bedroom all glitter and leopard print and killer silver boots. She tossed me a kiss and flopped down on the bed like she'd been gone minutes instead of days—the two longest days of my life.

I wanted to know where she'd been. Was it me? Had I done something wrong? But I didn't want to be *that* girl—Old Ellie—thinking everything everybody does has something to do with me.

"We need some music," she said, jumping up. She switched on the speakers, shuffling through my songs. "This one's my favorite," she said.

She played what was supposed to be The Last Song. A song by a band no one's heard of. The song I played when I tried to kill myself. It's not a song you can dance to, but Madeline did, circling the room, arms swinging, feet stomping, moving in a way I could never move without looking stupid. Madeline's dance was freaky and erratic, eerie almost. Not like those girls who look like they've stepped out of a music video—all pop and grind.

"It's my favorite, too," I said.

Madeline nodded like she knew. "Dance with me," she said. "It won't kill you." She smiled and wiggled and crooked her finger. I shook my head, but she reached down and dragged me across the floor by my foot until I gave in and got up.

I don't dance. I love music, but I don't have any rhythm. I don't look natural. But I didn't want to let Madeline down—didn't want her to leave. I started moving my feet in this slow, shuffling way, trying to be her—raising my arms over my head, letting my head hang low. My beast of a shadow lumbered clumsily and I wanted to vanish, to curl up under my bed and die. The song was building and building, reaching for the part where I'm huddled in my closet, pressing the cold blade to my wrist. I forced myself to keep moving.

Madeline's perfect blue eyes watched me carefully. Not in a judgmental way, not like Priscilla when she'd catch me singing or I'd read her a poem I'd written. (Was she ever really my friend?) She was watching me the way I'd watched her, like she wished she could be me. I know it's absurd. But I saw it, this desperate longing in her eyes, like she was aching for something hopeless. It felt weird. It wasn't right.

"I hate my body," I said.

Madeline grabbed my hands and said, "Don't ever say that again," and spun me around the room, faster and faster, until we were stumbling, tripping over our own feet, the heat radiating from our bodies making us dizzy. I've never taken drugs that make you feel good (painkillers, I guess), but I can imagine what it's like. There were kids at Jackson Middle who stole their parents' prescriptions (Valium, Oxycontin, Hydro-something) and took them or sold them, but I was never in that clique. Priscilla's part of that clique now. I wonder if she's taking drugs. I wonder if she knows what it's like to feel free and peaceful and confident. To feel at home in your own skin.

I dropped to the floor and Madeline quickly dropped, too. My long-sleeve shirt was drenched and my breathing hard. (God, I'm out of shape.) Between gasps, I asked, "Have you ever played knife?"

Madeline was winded, too. The hair at her temples was damp and spiky.

"You first," she said.

I was secretly happy when she circled her long, thin fingers around my wrist, but then I felt her thumb pressing against my scar. I knew I hadn't told her about that. Someday I'd tell her. Not today. Mom had said, over and over, when we get to Pottsville, don't publicize it. Keep it to yourself. Your new friends might not understand.

I pulled my arm free.

Where were my wrist bands? The black leather ones I'd bought online. Not the stupid rainbow ones Mom got me for gym. I started ransacking the room, tearing through drawers and boxes and bags. Madeline followed, trying to help. She was calling my name, but her voice was a million miles away. I'd fallen down a deep, dark hole.

"Whatever you're looking for—Stop, Ellie."

Madeline put her hands on my shoulders and sat me down on the bed. She had something to say, but I think she was deciding whether I was ready to hear it.

"We're the same," she whispered, and sat down next to me. "More than you know."

She pushed up her sleeves and turned her arms over and held them out for me to see. In that instant it felt like the world was collapsing and expanding all at once. I guess it was shock. Her veins looked so thin, so fragile, I wanted to cry. She had the whitest skin, but the scars were whiter still, whiter than sugar, whiter than marble. My poor stone angel.

Madeline's fingers circled my wrist again. This time I didn't resist. Slowly, gently, like I was something old and precious, she exposed my arm to the light. I closed my eyes and felt her breath on my skin—warm and soft—and then something warmer, softer. She'd pressed her lips against my scar. The blackness exploded in a million candy-colored pieces.

"It's like we're meant to be together," I said.

Madeline shook her head. "We *are* meant to be together."

"I want to know everything about you," I said.

"What's to know?"

I shrugged. "You know—"

"No, I don't." She went to the dresser and looked in the mirror. "What's it like to be you?"

"Me?" I said. "My life sucks."

Madeline shook her head. She pulled down her sleeves and turned off the music and stood before me looking beautiful and sad. Why do I always ruin everything? What exactly did I want to know? Stupid stuff, I guess. Does she have a boyfriend? What's her favorite movie? Has she ever tried a deep-fried candy bar? I should've asked something important, like why she tried to kill herself. Instead, I asked if she was popular. What a stupid question. Only someone who's not popular asks something like that.

Madeline shrugged. "I don't care about anyone else. I've got you."

Madeline's the most amazing girl I've ever met—inside and out. Which is rare. Beautiful people are usually obnoxious. She left before dark and now my dad is calling me for dinner. We spent all day together—Madeline and I—but I still don't know anything about her, not really. She's somehow just beyond my reach.

Does it matter? Do you ever really know another person? I thought I knew Priscilla, but I was wrong. I don't even know my own self. Six months ago, I thought I wanted to die. Now I know that I didn't. I wanted to escape. I was tired of my best friend acting like I didn't exist. One day I came home from school and thought, *I can't go back, I can't, I can't, I can't.* But you don't have many choices when you're fourteen. You can stand there and take it, or you can take your own life. I wanted a way out of Jackson Middle, and if that meant the world, too . . .

I know I'm not any of the things people think are important: athletic, pretty, smart. The list goes on and on. Not that I've never tried. My mother always said I lack stick-to-it-ive-ness. I give up too quickly. But that's not it. I'm not like other girls. I don't like what they like. I don't think about what they think about. I don't know what I want to be or how many kids I'm going to have or what I'm going to wear to the prom two years from now. My father thinks that's okay. According to him, I'm perfectly normal. He says I'll find myself.

I think I have. My purpose is clear. There's a reason why I survived the accident. Her name is Madeline Torus.

ten

Madeline Torus Madeline Torus Madeline Torus Madeline Torus
Madeline Torus Madeline Torus Madeline Torus Madeline Torus
Madeline Torus Madeline Torus Madeline Torus Madeline Torus
Madeline Torus Madeline Torus Madeline Torus Madeline Torus
Madeline Torus Madeline Torus Madeline Torus Madeline Torus
Madeline Torus Madeline Torus Madeline Torus Madeline Torus
Madeline Torus Madeline Torus Madeline Torus Madeline Torus
Madeline Torus Madeline Torus Madeline Torus Madeline Torus
Madeline Torus Madeline Torus Madeline Torus Madeline Torus
Madeline Torus Madeline Torus Madeline Torus Madeline Torus
Madeline Torus Madeline Torus Madeline Torus Madeline Torus
Madeline Torus Madeline Torus Madeline Torus Madeline Torus
Madeline Torus Madeline Torus Madeline Torus Madeline Torus
Madeline Torus Madeline Torus Madeline Torus

eleven

i don't have to be a fake around Madeline. I am what I am: Ellie Moss. Freak. Misfit. Loser. Whatever. I don't have to pretend to gush over the latest heartthrob or worry if my jeans taper or don't taper. Madeline doesn't care about cell phones or computers or if I have a pool. I'm not ashamed of my taste in music or poetry or my run-down house or my addiction to all things Pegasus. She doesn't think I'm a nothing because I've never kissed a boy or shoplifted makeup or dropped the F word in front of my parents. None of that stuff matters to her. To us.

Being friends with Priscilla was work. Which is funny because she was nothing special until Natalie Paquin decided she was. Her rise was so random. (It could've been anyone. It could've been me.) Priscilla was in the right place at the right time. If she hadn't been out walking her mangy dog past the car wash when that creepy guy tried to grab Natalie, none of what happened would've happened. Natalie would've made a beautiful corpse in an abandoned lot, and Scilla and I would've stayed friends forever. Instead, my best friend saved the school's biggest snob, and the two of them became inseparable. The next thing I knew, Priscilla was hanging out with Natalie instead of me. She was getting contact lenses. She was letting Brandon Clark feel her up behind the bleachers.

"She's still the same person," I said. "Shallow, pathetic, a total airhead."

"Keep going," Madeline said. She stretched out next to me on the bed where I'd been sitting for the last hour, chin on my knees, replaying The Worst Year of My Life.

"You want to hear all this?" I said.

"Sure." She looked at me with those big blue eyes. "You need to get it off your chest. You can't let it eat at your soul."

She was right. I'd never told anyone how I felt about Priscilla, how much I hated her. Not that there was anyone to tell. But if there were, I would've been afraid to burn that bridge. In my mind there was always a spark of hope, the remotest possibility that Priscilla would realize she'd lost the truest friend she'd ever had.

Fat chance.

A week ago I could not have said what I said this afternoon. All the loathing and disgust and anger flowed out of my heart. It's amazing all the things you find to hate about a person when that person becomes your enemy—things that never bothered you when that person was your friend. Like Priscilla's tuna breath. Or the way she walked like an elephant and spoke baby talk with her mother in public. I hated that she borrowed clothes and gave them back stained and smelling like her dog. Or how she said "prolly" instead of "probably."

When I finished, Madeline smiled. "Feel better?" she said.

And I did. All the cruel thoughts leaving me felt good.

"Maybe I'd feel even better if I wrote her a letter," I said. "She deserves to hear what I think about her. Worse, really."

Madeline rolled over on her stomach. "Why? She lives in another world."

She was right. She'd just throw it out, or she'd run to Natalie.

Priscilla: Is my laugh really that bad? I don't sound like a
    hyena, do I?
Natalie: Elanor Moss is a freak. She's jealous of you.
Priscilla: You're prolly right.

It wouldn't be like it was for me. *I* didn't have anyone to turn to. *I* didn't have a shoulder to cry on. Scilla was my one-and-only and when she abandoned me, I had no one. Not a single friend.

But none of that matters anymore. Madeline is my world now. We've known each other only a few days and already we're finishing each other's sentences. Scilla and I were always going places: her house, my house, the library, the cemetery, the mall. Always bored. Always searching for something, anything to keep from going crazy. We don't go anywhere—Madeline and I—but I don't care. We have everything we want right here in my room: We have each other.

I'm never lonely anymore. When Madeline's not here, I have my mother. It's funny how I feel closer to her now that she's dead. When she was alive, I was always pushing her away, acting like she was annoying, a pain I just barely tolerated. I wish she could read this. Can she read this? Are you reading this right now? I can feel you stroking that soft spot behind my ear. You used to do that when I was little, to calm me down after a nightmare. I love you. You know that, right?

You would've loved Madeline. She's smart and fun and beautiful—all the things I'm not. I know you'd disagree. You believed in potential. You believed in choices. (Sorry, Mom, but no one chooses to be stupid or ugly or weird.) "It's all just a matter of nurturing your good qualities," you'd say, "dialing down the negative self-talk. You have to learn to love yourself."

I didn't always love myself. But now I do. I love who I am around Madeline. We're complete opposites, but when I'm with her I feel whole. Yesterday I tried to explain how I felt, and she told me this amazing story about some ancient Greek philosopher who believed that humans used to have four arms and four legs and two faces. We were these perfectly happy roly-poly creatures, but the gods thought we were too powerful, so they split everyone in two, condemning us to spend eternity searching for our other perfect half.

I don't know where she gets this stuff. She said she learned it in school. I probably did, too, but I don't remember. I was either too busy trying to survive or trying to die. That's another thing that used to upset my mother—grades. "If I thought you were developmentally disabled (translation: retarded), I would be proud of all these Cs. You're a bright girl, Ellie. I expect more." Good Grades was on the New Beginning list. I guess it still is, but who's going to care? My father? He hardly notices me now.

I think about you a lot, Mommy—all the time, really. I can't get my head around the fact that I'll never see you again. Probably because I can still feel you. I can't decide if it's a good thing. If what I'm feeling isn't you, but some trick of my damaged brain, then it's probably bad. But if it is you, I don't ever want you to let go.

I've been trying to tell Madeline about you. I don't know why I've waited so long. Probably because of the way Daddy reacted.

I know Madeline is different, but I also know how it sounds: "Oh, by the way . . . my dead mother . . . she's not really gone. I mean, she holds my hand—she's holding my hand right now." But I'm not crazy, you're here. You have to be.

I love Madeline. I trust her with everything—my life, even. But this is weird. I hate keeping you a secret from my best friend. I'm not ashamed or embarrassed, it's just that this feels incredibly private. More than the box of Old Ellie journals stashed under the bed. More than the scars on my wrists. It'd be like Madeline and I rifling through Daddy's wallet. Worse. It'd be like telling her about when you two almost split up and I found Daddy crying in your lap, with you rocking him, hushing him like a baby.

I've probably already told her about you. I still have memory lapses. I know what Madeline wore three days ago (camouflage tank, shredded tutu, those amazing silver boots), but I don't remember what Daddy fed me for dinner tonight. (Something from a can, most likely.) Or when it started raining. It's really coming down right now, drumming the porch roof outside my window, pinging the gutters. The wind whips the tree out front, whistling in the eaves. There's a leak in my ceiling, right over my desk. The spot swells, getting larger and larger. A drop tugs loose and lands on my photo of Lucy. My eyes drift for something to catch the next one. Instead they flicker to a figure at the window, dark and crouched, reaching a long, pale hand . . .

It's the middle of the night. The ceiling is still leaking, but there's a pencil cup under it now. Earlier I thought I was hallucinating. Ghostly fingers tapped the glass. A drowned white face swam up out of the darkness. But it was just Madeline, soaked and shivering, whispering to be let in. The frame is still painted shut, so I motioned for her to go around the side, to the bathroom. The window is smaller, but it opens. She squeezed through, wiggled over the sill, and flopped down on the floor.

"You scared the crap out of me!" I said, grabbing a towel from the rack to dry her hair.

"I missed you."

I shook my head and hugged her and took her to the kitchen for something to eat. Madeline is crazy. I would never have the guts to sneak out. I could never do anything without my mother knowing. My father's a different story. Asleep on the couch, he didn't even hear us tiptoe through the living room, giggling and shivering like he was some evil ogre waiting to reach out and snap our bones. We raided the cupboards for cheese-filled pretzels for me and cookies for her, and ran back upstairs to sit on my bed and stuff our faces and dream about what it would be like to live together forever.

And now here we are, side by side, Madeline sleeping soundly, her hair fanned over my pillow. I can feel her breath on my elbow. The heat radiating from her body warms me all over. Blue veins streak her temples, reminding me of those other veins—the ones in her wrists, the ones she tried to sever—because she was sad and lonely, just like me. But she's safe now. I would never hurt her, not in a million years. Not my Madeline. My stone angel. I will always be hers. She will always be mine. Forever and ever. She is more than a friend, she's a part of me. Watching her sleep, my heart aches in a good way. She makes me happy to be alive. These days with her are like a dream. When we're together, there is no past, no future, only now, the two of us in my room. Nothing else matters. When I think of all the things that could have kept us apart . . . I'm not going to write about it. I can't write about it. Not now. Not ever.

twelve

My father and I had a fight this morning. Maybe "fight" isn't the right word. It was pretty one-sided, with me ranting and raving while my father gazed blankly at me. It all started with the leak above my desk. This morning there was a giant ugly stain. I'd swapped the pencil cup for the wastebasket, but it had rained all night and the leak had shifted. Now everything on my desk is wet and ruined.

"At least it wasn't over your bed." My father's pathetic attempt at humor. I was not amused.

"How long are we going to live like this?" I said, swinging my arms at the unpacked boxes, the trash piling up in the corner, the tangle of sheets strewn over my father's makeshift bed on the couch. Even with its leaky ceiling, my room is an oasis.

My father lowered his head in shame. He always played the role of the child with my mother, expecting her to pick up the pieces of our broken lives. And now he's doing it with me, oblivious to everything but his own pain. He didn't even know Madeline slept over.

My father started to walk away.

"You're the adult here!" I screamed. "Act like one!"

My stomach dropped. I froze. My father has never hit me, but I half expected him to march over and slap my face. Holler at me, at least, in his scary dad voice: *Lose the attitude, Elanor!* But he just shook his head sadly, fixing me with those empty eyes.

It made me even angrier.

"When are you going to start your new job?" I said. "When are you going to get the phone and cable turned on? I don't even have clothes to start school!"

He ran his hand over his face and then fiddled with the tie on his robe. He looked tired, unbelievably tired. "Give me a couple of days," he said.

"Days? You've had weeks! Mommy's not coming back! You're not going to wake up one morning and find her sitting at the kitchen table making her lists! Don't you get it? She's dead!"

And that's when I went and dredged up the past, poking my finger in old wounds. I needed a sign he's still here—that he hasn't checked out for good.

"I see why she wanted to leave you," I hissed. "She was tired of trying to do everything by herself! I'd leave if I could!"

My father stood there blinking. If that didn't faze him, nothing would. He was gone, completely. All my anger drained away, and I was filled with the most awful realization: I haven't just lost my mother . . . I've lost my father, too.

"This is only temporary," he said.

"What's temporary? The boxes and trash and canned food? Our life—if you can call *this* a life—in Pottsville? This ocean of sorrow?"

My father crooked his finger for me to listen carefully.

"*Everything* is temporary," he whispered. His breath smelled like ashes. I winced.

Those three little words sent me plummeting over the edge. Stumbling, as if I'd been hit, I reached to steady myself and knocked my mother's favorite lamp to the floor. The base cracked in two, and the bulb exploded into a million pieces. The ground was slipping beneath my feet. Gravity had stopped working. If I didn't get down on my hands and knees, I'd fly right off the face of the earth.

In my soul I know he's right. Everything is temporary. Look at my mother. You think your parents are as constant as the moon in the sky, but they're not.

"Let's do something permanent."

That's what Madeline said after she held my head in her lap and let me cry about my dad and then cried with me when I told her I was afraid of losing her, too.

"I'm not going anywhere," she said. "Not without you."

I want to believe her, but she's not immortal. She could burn up in a fire. She could tumble down a flight of stairs and snap her neck. It seems like something the gods from her story would do: Give me Madeline and then snatch her away.

"We'll need something sharp," she said, poking through my dresser. "A small knife or a razor."

I figured she wanted to carve something, our names, maybe, into my desk or the floorboards or the tree outside my window. I was shocked when she said, "We'll need some ice, too, to numb ourselves. And some towels and some gauze and tape."

In the old days, I would've had to slink around the house to hide what I was doing. My mother was always spying on Scilla and me, suspicious of everything. Not my father.

Me: Where's the box cutter?
Dad: Kitchen counter.
Me: First-aid kit?
Dad: Check the bathroom.

"What do you think of this?" Madeline asked. She was sitting on the bed, a pad of paper in her lap, sketching. She turned the pad around and showed me two upside-down *v*'s, side by side, next to two lazy *v*'s stacked one over the other. I loved it. It was simple and perfect. No ampersand separating us. No plus sign. Our sum is greater than our parts:

$$\text{M}\epsilon$$

"Take off your shirt," she said.

I flinched. Even with all the weight I've lost, I'm still fat in the middle.

Madeline rolled her eyes. "You have to. It's nothing I haven't seen."

I peeled my shirt over my head and stood there shivering in my bra. Madeline pressed the ice-filled towel to my chest, over my heart. The cold took my breath away.

"I promise it won't hurt," she said, raising the blade. I lifted my face to the ceiling. I couldn't watch. I still feel sick when I remember cutting my wrists—the raw, hot suddenness of steel slicing through skin. I locked my knees and dug my nails into my palms, bracing for the kaleidoscope of pain. I didn't want to jerk and screw it up. I was breathing hard, still wondering what she was waiting for, when she pressed a gauze pad to my skin and said, "There. Done." I wouldn't have believed it if I hadn't seen the bloody letters seeping through the white square.

"I told you I wouldn't hurt you," she said, handing me the silver blade. "Don't hurt me."

Madeline is sleeping over again. She's lounging in bed, flipping through a book my English teacher assigned for the poetry unit last year. I liked it so much, I borrowed it—forever. Madeline just read me one by the guy who uses all lowercase letters. He's one of my favorites. I've read it before. I love the last line: *i carry your heart (i carry it in my heart).* Madeline pulled down her collar and showed me her bandage. I showed her mine.

She read a few more and then scooted down under the covers like a little kid waiting for a bedtime story. I told her to pick a poem and I'd read it to her, but she wants to hear something by me. She wants to hear something from my journal.

"What do you write about?" she asks.

How can I answer her truthfully? I write about everything. My dead mother. My messed-up father. My messed-up brain. Love. Scilla. The horror of dying. Busted windshields and leaky ceilings. Betrayal. Stone angels. Canned soup. Car wrecks. Monsters and black holes and gods.

The list goes on and on.

I don't ever read my own words. Because I never get it right, what I'm trying to say. It always falls short. I know good writing when I read it. Good writing makes my heart feel like a soda bottle that's been shaken, the pressure building and building, until I think I might explode into a million tiny pieces. The poet who stuck her head in an oven makes me feel that way. I'll read something from her instead.

thirteen

his morning I went through a box marked MINE. It was all
my mother's personal things, stuff she didn't just leave
around the house, stuff she kept separate from my stuff and my
dad's stuff: her high school yearbook, a dried rose from her mother's casket, my baby teeth, a ticket stub from a concert in 1988, a
bunch of letters and postcards and homemade Mother's Day
cards, and two grainy black-and-white photos on thin, filmy paper. I put everything else back carefully except the photos. Those
I kept.

They were ultrasound images of me in my mother's womb,
but in the first photo—the one labeled 8 WEEKS—I wasn't alone.
The images were eerie, almost alien, with two black voids in a
sea of variegated gray. In the first one, both voids contained a
single white bean. In the second photo, the bean on the left had
grown but the bean on the right was missing. The right void
had shrunk to a pinhole, crowded out by the void on the left.

"What are you doing?" It was my father. He'd appeared out of nowhere, startling me. I hid the pictures in my pocket.

"I'm looking for the camera," I said.

"It's not in there." He stormed over and closed the flaps. Obviously my father isn't ready to have me nosing through my mother's things. He hefted the box and marched off.

"Do you know where it is?" I called after him.

"Try the blue tub."

The blue tub was next to the couch. My father had been using it as a nightstand. The top was cluttered with drinking glasses and used tissues. I pried off the lid and peered inside. The camera bag was buried in a nest of Christmas lights.

It isn't a very good camera. It's cheap plastic and the directions that came with it suck. Mom was always accidentally deleting pictures. I pressed the power button and the preview screen lit up. There was my mom and me packing up our old house. Then this house—the one in Pottsville—taken back in June when the Realtor had given us a walk-through. There was my dad posing on the front porch, and me with a wicked case of red-eye, looking possessed. And then there was the picture I'd taken of Mom in the yard, kneeling beside an overgrown rosebush, the sun framing her hair in gold. She hadn't noticed me standing in the driveway, trying to get the stupid zoom to work. She looks so happy in that picture, so peaceful, lifting a yellow bud to her nose. But was she? Life had failed her in so many ways. Correction: *We* had failed her in so many ways.

Madeline was still in bed, exactly as I'd left her: curled on her side, arm under her head. I'd spent the last hour studying her face. I couldn't pull my eyes away. It was how I used to get around Scilla's father when he didn't have his shirt pinned around his stump. I felt that if I looked long enough—if the light was right and I could get closer—I'd see how she was created, I'd learn the secret of what made Madeline Madeline. Is that weird? Probably. That's what I was thinking when Madeline's eyes fluttered open. She smiled at the camera and shook her hair and rolled out of bed.

"Delete that," she said.

"I want a picture of you," I said. "A nice one. Not one of those crappy school ones."

Madeline pulled on a skirt and a top and went and stood in front of the closet. "Is this good?" she said. I was about to press the silver button when . . . I don't know what. I guess I blacked out. I was getting ready to take the picture, and then I was slumped on the bed. I don't know how long I'd been like that. Madeline was curled up in the corner, shivering and wild-eyed. Her pupils were huge, like the two black voids in the ultrasound. She looked like she'd seen something terrible. From behind her back she pulled a black-and-white composition book—this journal. She'd been reading my journal.

"Doesn't this mean anything to you?" she said, peeling back the bandage over her heart. The letters were a bloody brown. The surrounding skin looked burned. The cuts on my chest began itching and stinging.

"Of course it does," I said.

"Then why didn't you tell me?"

Tell her what? What was in my journal that I hadn't told her?

"The stuff about your mother."

My ears burned. I jumped up, knocking the camera to the floor. The flash went off. I started stuttering like an idiot.

"It's just—It's true," I said. "Not in some cheesy metaphorical way. She really holds my hand. Sometimes she kisses my forehead. Sometimes she plays with my hair. I didn't know how to tell you that her ghost—" I stopped. I hadn't ever used that term to describe my mother. Not even in my head. It's not the right word. I don't know what to call her.

"I wanted to tell you," I whispered.

Madeline crawled across the floor and sat on her knees. She looked down at her lap and said, "This changes everything." At first I thought she was angry. But it wasn't anger. It was fear. Her voice was full of deep concern. Panic, almost.

"It's not a bad thing," I said. "Having her around makes me feel better."

"You miss your mother. I understand. But you can't cling—"

"No. It's probably nothing. Just my screwed-up brain."

Madeline covered her face, but I just stood there next to her, staring down, afraid to open my mouth and make it worse.

"You don't understand," she said. "It's just . . . there's a plan. Never mind. Sit." She patted the rug and reached for my hand—my mother's hand—and calmly folded my fingers.

"Everything will be all right," she said softly. "We'll figure this out. Concentrate. Concentrate."

Clutching my fist, she squeezed. Gently at first, but then hard, harder.

"Madeline's crying," she chanted. "Elanor's dying. Concentrate. Concentrate."

Her grip tightened. I winced but she kept squeezing.

"Madeline's dying. Elanor's crying."

Her hands were a vise. Tighter and tighter, she squeezed. Like she was trying to halt the blood pouring from a wound. Like she was trying to fuse us together. My knuckles popped like bubble wrap. A sickening shifting of bones. I gritted my teeth and blinked back a wave of tears.

Something snapped. My stomach lurched. Madeline felt it,

too, and dropped my fist like it was toxic. "I can't feel her," she whispered. "I have to go."

My hand has stopped hurting, but everything else is on fire—my head, my stomach, my heart, the initials I let her carve into my flesh. It feels like the gauze is infested with ants, biting and stinging, tunneling into my chest. What is wrong with me? What was I thinking? Why didn't I tell her about my mother? This is what I wrote, this is what she read:

I'm not ashamed or embarrassed,
it's just this feels incredibly private.

Incredibly stupid is more like it. I spent The Worst Year of My Life aching for someone who's honest and loyal and sees things the same way. Someone who loved me for me. Someone who made me feel whole. Just when I thought my life would never change, Madeline comes along, appearing out of nowhere like some guardian angel (my stone angel), and this is how I repay her? By keeping secrets?

And now I have another one.

I pull the two crumpled photos from my pocket and smooth them out on the desk.

I don't know what it means.

fourteen

I have two settings: hot and cold. My mother used to say that no one can accuse me of being lukewarm. I'm up and down like a yo-yo. Life is all rainbows or it's a stinking heap of garbage.

Today it is rainbows.

"Look who I found," Madeline said, dumping an orange-and-white cat—my cat, Lucy Cat—on the rug. I dropped to my knees and scooped her up and tossed her over my shoulder. I buried my nose in her fur and smelled her Lucy smell—dust and canned food and saliva. I thought only old people cried tears of joy. I guess I've never been this happy.

We'd lost her in the Poconos, over a hundred miles from Pottsville. I've heard of animals traveling farther, but Lucy's old and she's a house cat. How did she survive? You'd think a cat who had crossed mountains and rivers and a state line would come limping in all bloody paws and matted fur, ribs sticking out—but she looked perfectly healthy.

I asked Madeline how she found her.

"I have my ways."

I wiped my eyes. My nose was running, too. "No, really," I said.

"About yesterday," she said. "I'm sorry. I guess I'm a little possessive. Okay, a lot possessive."

My mother was right about so many things. (Hear that, Mom, you were right.) I give up too quickly. I get that from you-know-who. Last night I cried myself to sleep thinking Madeline hated me, and that I'd never see her again, and then she comes here asking *me* to forgive *her*. The same with Lucy. I could've found her if I'd tried. Madeline did. It wasn't magic. There's this thing called a newspaper. There's this thing called the Internet. I just figured she was dead. Why do I find hope so difficult? My answer to everything is to curl up into a little ball and wait for the world to end. Good things do happen for Ellie. Not always, but sometimes.

I just fed Lucy a can of tuna for her homecoming dinner. Now she's racing around my room, stalking a pen cap. I wonder when my father's coming home. That was another surprise: My father left the house. He's been gone all day. This morning, before it was light, he came into my room, kissed the top of my head, and said, "I love you, Ellie. I'm going now." Where? I don't know. Work, I guess. He was wearing a suit and tie. His breath smelled like ashes. Is he smoking again? I want to show him Lucy. I want to ask him about the ultrasounds, too, before I show them to Madeline. It's dark and he's still not home.

fifteen

i don't remember seeing my father today. It doesn't mean I didn't—I just don't remember. I'm sick. Lucy's sick. My body is fighting something, a cold or the flu. I've been asleep more than I've been awake and feel prickly all over. There's also this weird hot fluttering in my chest, like a tiny flaming bird trapped behind my ribs. I tried taking my temperature, but the thermometer's broken—I can't get a reading. And my cuts might be infected. They itch like crazy. It takes all my willpower to keep from clawing at the stupid bandage. Then there's my psycho cat. She's been crouched at the foot of the bed all day, making that strangled calling noise she makes when she can't find me. "Hello?" I wiggle my toes. "I'm right here, dummy."

All I want to do is sleep, but Madeline won't let me. It's like she's afraid I might slip into a coma and never regain consciousness. Every time I close my eyes, she asks another question.

The last one: "Are you happy right here, right now?"

"I feel like crap," I said. "But yeah. Why?"

"I'm afraid part of you wants your old life back. Your life before the accident."

Why would she say such a thing? For the first time in a long time, I am truly happy. I don't want to die. I'd give anything to be with my mother again, but my mother is dead and I want to live. Madeline wants me to prove something. I don't know what. It's some kind of test. If I could reverse time and save my mother, I would. But I can't.

There's only one answer: "No."

"Good," she said. And then like one had something to do with the other, "I want you to go somewhere with me."

"Sure," I said. I've been shut up in this house—what?—fifteen, sixteen days. I need to buy clothes for school. I'd kill to see a movie. But that's not what she meant. She wants to run away. The two of us. Far from here. She said it's time to start over. Everything's ready. Our new life is waiting.

"Where?" I said.

"A different world. One where we can be together forever."

This is my chance to prove how much I love her. It's an easy choice. I'll still have my mother. She's more alive to me than my father. He won't even notice I'm gone.

Madeline won't let me in on any of the details. She said it's a secret. I don't know what she's planning. She said I can't bring anything. Not a bag. Not my journal. Not even Lucy.

sixteen

Lucy's been making that calling noise for two days. Now her voice is gone. Her mouth moves but nothing comes out. It's funny and sad at the same time. I think she feels my mom's presence and it's got her all freaked out. They say animals are sensitive like that, to things people can't hear or see or feel.

Whatever I've got is getting worse. I'm weak. Too weak to write. We're leaving tomorrow. Or the next day.

seventeen

I'm not taking this with me. Maybe my father will find it someday and understand.

I'll never know what happened to the baby.

(People crying. Babies dying.)

Elanor's dying. Madeline's crying. Madeline kisses me on the lips. Not like a boy. Closer. We are meant to be forever. Something flutters at the window. Birds. Blackbirds. Black as ash. They think I am trapped, but I'm not. We're leaving. It's raining. Won't our feathers get wet?

The ceiling is leaking. The house is crumbling. The birds are lurking in the trees, rattling the windows, pecking my brain. My brain is shrinking. Everything's shrinking. I'm shivering. I'm shivering silver stars. It's raining metal and plastic.

I'm drowning. My lungs are bursting. Madeline wants me to follow her, but it's dark where she's going. I must brave the darkness to enter the light. She's building a nest with twigs and sticks. I hear the charred birds in the charred trees, calling: *Mine. Mine.* Something tugs at my ankles. The ground is slipping. Everything is slipping.

Madeline's dying, Elanor's crying.

I fear black. I fear light. Birds calling: *Mine! Mine!*

part ii
the pegasus journal

All we are not stares back at what we are.
—W. H. Auden

*t*he doctor said I'm a fighter. He said I had one foot in the grave. The force of the impact caused a subdural hematoma. (Translation: a bruised brain.) He said that's why I'm seeing things, these weird shadows. I'm lucky I'm not a vegetable. If I follow orders and don't have any setbacks, I can go home on Monday. But what home? I feel like I've been asleep forever. Everything is still pretty sketchy. I'm in a hospital in the Poconos. An RV swooped down like some giant terrible bird and destroyed our car. I asked my mother if my father went on to Pottsville, to start his new job. She said I should try some Jell-O.

"Daddy's dead," I said. "Isn't he?"

My mother pinched her nose like she was stifling a sneeze. She nodded.

"Lucy, too?"

Another nod. A sniff. She wouldn't let herself cry. Not in front of me.

I leaned back against the pillow and closed my eyes, trying to picture my dad. But I just kept seeing him buried beneath a pile of blankets on the couch in our new house. Not our old house. Not behind the wheel of our car, joking about locking me in the cat carrier. Not at the last stop before the accident, when I'd pinched him for taking a big bite out of my ice cream. That's how I wanted to remember him, but I couldn't. My heart hurt worse than my head. I wanted to scream, but I felt someone hovering, leaning over me. I opened my eyes. A shadow wrapped me in its arms, drawing the pain from my chest. I tried to hold on, but it slipped over the side of the bed. The black shape rose up against the door—a girl, definitely a girl—and then she was gone.

"Wait," I said. "I know you."

"Know who?" my mother said.

"The girl. We were going somewhere together."

My mother hadn't seen her. It was nothing. My eyes playing tricks. My messed-up brain.

"Let's think about you right now." My mother squeezed my hand. "Focus on getting you well."

nineteen

he clock over the sink read 1:08. The drapes on the window were drawn shut. There's a button I can push when I need help. Every once in awhile a nurse will bustle in and check my chart and help me to the bathroom or get me a drink of water or give me another pain pill if it's time. But I haven't used the button. Swinging my legs over the edge of the bed, I planted my feet heavily on the cold tile floor. Reaching back, I held my gown closed in a fist as I crossed the room to open the drapes. The blackness beyond made the window a mirror. There's a big purple bruise on my forehead. My lips are dry and cracked. I've got some cuts and scratches and more bruises, but otherwise I look pretty much the same as I did before the accident. My face is too round. My hair is too short. I pulled the gown tighter and stood up straight. Same bulge in the middle where my waist should be. Maybe it was the painkillers talking, but I thought, *I'm okay with a little fat.* My hair will grow in before school. I let go of the gown, smiling at myself and running my tongue over my teeth. I was about to search for a toothbrush when something in the reflection of the fluorescent-lit room caught my eye. The shadow again. In the corner, behind the door, where the lights don't reach. A grainy black void hunched and waiting. I froze, my eyes and ears straining.

A voice, but not really. More like a radio stuck between stations. Slowly, one channel teased from the static, rising, shivering until I heard clearly:

Hey there, it's me.

My heart slammed against my ribs. I spun around. Standing in the doorway was the night orderly, the one with the superhero scrubs, pushing a stainless steel cart.

"What do you want?" I said. "What did you say?"

His eyes narrowed with concern for the girl with the bruised brain. "I'm here if you need me."

twenty

this is how we started the ride to our new home: my father behind the wheel of our crappy little hatchback, my mother on the passenger side, me squished in back with Lucy in her carrier and a pillow and a blanket and a big bag of snacks.

This is how we ended it: my mother driving a shiny new rental, me riding shotgun, my father in an urn in a box in the trunk.

My mother pulled into the driveway and turned off the headlights and sighed, the release deflating her, as if she'd been holding her breath since Pennsylvania. I guess I had, too. Every lane change, every merge, every tug of the brakes flooded my system with adrenaline. We sat there awhile, silently watching the moon over the woods behind the house. The idea of climbing out of the car and opening the front door was too much. I wanted to stay where I was, not thinking, not moving, listening to the rhythmic tick of the engine cooling, the chirping of crickets, the slow, steady whisper of my mother drawing air into her lungs.

"You ready?" she asked quietly. She reached across the darkness and squeezed my hand. I squeezed back. My mother grabbed her purse and I grabbed my bag. The suitcases we left for later. My father, too. The sensor light came on and we followed the gravel path to the porch. My mother unlocked the door and flipped the switch. I'd seen the house before, once back in June when the real estate agent had given us a tour. But walking into the house tonight was like walking into a dream. I don't know how to explain it. It was the same feeling I would've had if we'd turned around in Pennsylvania and gone back to our old house in Jackson. It was the feeling of coming home—but not to a new house. I already lived here. Everything looked eerily familiar, like something I'd seen in an old photo: the towers of boxes and tubs, the furniture scattered around the living room, my mother's favorite lamp in pieces. *The lamp.* A shock of guilt as I remembered it breaking. My mother shook her head at the mess.

"Sorry," I said.

My mother shrugged. "Insurance'll pay for it." She picked up the bigger pieces and shuffled off to the kitchen, turning on lights as she went. The house was what my parents had called a "fixer-upper." When we'd seen it in June, it had been empty. I remembered it feeling small and echoey. It had smelled like it had been shut up for a long time, like mice and basement and stale crackers. It didn't smell like that anymore. Maybe it was all our stuff, but the house smelled like our family now, like my father's aftershave and Lucy's cat breath and my shampoo.

In the kitchen, my mother was going through a stack of mail. There was a basket of fruit on the counter. "The real estate agent," she said, showing me the card. She'd stocked our fridge, too, with milk, eggs, and orange juice. I ate an apple. I was tired and hungry and my head was killing me. I wanted to go to bed and wake up and find that all of this was just a bad dream. I wanted to open my eyes and see Lucy at the foot of my bed. I wanted to go downstairs in the morning and find my parents making breakfast in our new kitchen.

"Let's go upstairs," my mother said. "I've got a surprise for you."

The air on the second floor was heavy with fumes. "I hired a painter," she said, opening the door to the room I'd picked during the walk-through. It was just like Mom to think ahead—planning, doing—while the world was crumbling at her feet.

"I hope you like it. They're your colors. Nacho Cheese and Chips, right?" She shaded her eyes and grimaced. "It's awfully bright."

I scanned the room. It was exactly as I'd remembered. Correction: not remembered. It wasn't a memory. It couldn't be. It was exactly as I'd imagined. My bed was against the far wall, my desk and dresser at opposite ends, a bunch of boxes marked ELLIE neatly stacked beside the closet. My books, my dollhouse, my Pegasus collection, everything was exactly where I'd . . . I don't know.

It's overwhelming—not the color—the feeling. The deep knowing. I felt the room spinning, slipping. I felt light-headed. I stumbled and said, "I don't feel good."

"Sit," my mother said. "I'll let some air in here."

"The window won't open," I said.

My mother looked confused but tried anyway. I was right. It was painted shut. My mother looked around for something and then looked up and frowned. Above the desk an ugly bloom, the color of dead flowers. A water stain through the fresh paint. She climbed on the chair and stretched her arm above her head and felt for dampness.

"When did that happen?" she said.

"I told Daddy—"

My mother missed it. She went on: "That needs to be fixed." She hopped down and dusted her hands. "I'm not going to worry about it tonight. I've got to find the sheets."

"I'm going to get changed," I said.

She brushed back my hair and examined the bruise on my forehead. "Are you okay?"

I wasn't, but I needed to be alone. I bobbed my head and smiled. She wouldn't leave if she thought I was sick.

"Shout if you need me," she said, her hand on the doorknob. "I'll be downstairs."

I sat on the bare mattress and wondered how I knew what I knew: the busted lamp. The water stain above my desk. The stuck window. I hadn't checked yet, but I knew one of the fluorescent tubes in the bathroom flickers and hums. It didn't make sense. It wasn't possible. *Exhaustion,* I thought. *Grief. My bruised brain.*

I tugged on sweatpants and took the long way to the kitchen—through the living room, past the dining room, down the dark hall that leads to a windowless back room. I turned on the light. My father was in his study. My mother had brought him in from the car. He always needed more space than the rest of us, a place where he could be alone when his heavy-hearted moods struck. I wondered what we'd do with the room now. I wondered what we'd do with my father. My mother had him cremated in Pennsylvania. Now we have to find somewhere to bury his ashes. We could just leave the urn on the big oak desk—it's not like it's bothering anybody—but knowing my mother, she already has a plot picked out.

I turned off the light and backtracked to the kitchen. My mother was at the table, staring blankly into a cup of tea. My mom has always looked younger than other moms. She's in shape and dresses nice and always wears makeup, even when she's sick, even when she cleans house. But right then, under the bright kitchen light, she looked older, with deep lines etched into her forehead and finer lines radiating from her eyes. Normally my mother's the most expressive person you'll ever meet. She's always smiling or frowning or screwing up her face in a way that makes me angry or makes me laugh, depending on my mood. It was weird seeing her face silent.

"We're gonna be okay," I said.

My mother looked up, smiling tightly, and blew on her tea. "I know." She nodded confidently, but her red-rimmed eyes betrayed her.

I'm sorry I've hurt her. Not that the accident was my fault. But her suffering started long before that RV went crashing through the guardrail, because of me. I wanted her to know that her hope wasn't wasted. It's what saved me, kept me tethered to this world. She's the reason I'm still here. "You held my hand the whole time I was in the hospital," I said. It wasn't a question but a statement. Another one of those things I just knew.

My mother put down the teacup. "I never left your side," she said.

"We're gonna be okay," I said again. "Better than okay."

"It's good to hear you say that."

My mother went to bed about an hour ago. By the way, have I said how much I love my new journal? The old one was lost in the accident. It's probably in a ditch somewhere. Mom got this one in the hospital gift shop. I'm used to writing in those marble compositions, but this is a real book, with a silver Pegasus on the cover and a ribbon to mark your page.

I'm jonesing for a bag of cheese-filled pretzels. New Ellie's eating a banana instead. I like fruit, but it doesn't fill me. I meant what I said in the kitchen. Mom and I can make this work. It's still our New Beginning. Things will be different without Dad, but maybe, in some way . . . I almost can't even write it . . . it's better that Mom was the one who survived. I don't think my father could've handled losing her. It'll be hard, but we'll make it—my mom and me. The doctor called me a fighter. I get that from her.

I do have to say it's weird having him downstairs. His ashes, that is. Part of me wants to go down and sit with him. But I know it's not my father, just his body reduced to dust. Plus, there's this other part of me that feels like we've said good-bye. We were together after the accident, before I came to in the hospital bed. The doctor said I had one foot in the grave. I know he didn't mean literally, but what if I did? It would explain this memory that can't be a memory of me and my father. I know I sound crazy. It's not like we were romping through fields of wildflowers. No wings or white flowing gowns. No trumpets. No pearl-encrusted gates. We were here. We lived in this house, my father and I. It's like our souls, or whatever, came here to rest after the accident, until I got called back to this world and he went to wherever it is you go when you die. Heaven, I guess. We're not really religious, our family. The last time I saw my father, I was in this bed, in this room. He was wearing a suit and tie. His breath smelled like ashes. I remember he kissed me good-bye. I remember he told me he loved me. I remember someone else, too. The shadow girl from the hospital. Memories swoop in, peck at my brain, and then scatter. There's this sadness hanging over everything. I feel it now, but it's not my father. It's her. She wants to tell me something, but this fog in my head is thick and blinding. It's like following a voice through a flaming forest.

twenty-one

this shadow is my friend. No. The connection runs deeper than friendship. She's here in my room. We're separated by something clear and smooth and bright. A mirror. A lake. She's rising toward the surface. Closer. Reaching. Reaching for me. I study my palm as if it holds the answer. Something pricks my heart when I think of her. Our souls converge at the edge of sleep, but I am wide awake. When I'm awake, my body resists, my brain questions it. But not for long. I took one of the pills the doctor prescribed for my mother to help her get some rest.

twenty-two

My mother says we're going through an Adjustment Period. We need routine. It's like boot camp around here. Up at seven. Showers and beds made by eight. Yogurt and fruit for breakfast. Salad for lunch. Tons and tons of water. I know it's good for me, but I'm in the bathroom every five minutes.

When we're not peeing, cleaning up the yard, or unpacking the house, we go to the bigger small town for groceries and stuff. Sometimes we drive the extra twenty miles to the city. There's a sad little mall and a home improvement store and a warehouse club and a shiny strip of fast-food places where we never get to eat. We're there to gather things from The List. Up and down the aisles we go, checking things off: bales of paper products, monster jugs of fat-free dressing, things to fix our house. It needs a lot of work, but right now it's totally livable. My mother could make a cardboard box homey.

We're on a tight schedule because school starts in two weeks—for me and for Mom. Four nights a week she'll be taking classes for her real estate license. She wants to get it done in six months, before the life insurance money runs out. Next week we'll bury my father. Tomorrow we'll go look at cars. Today we painted my mother's room. I went up on the ladder with a brush and cut in along the top where the wall meets the ceiling, but I kept dripping paint.

"Shit," I said, gazing down at the violet splotches on the hardwood floor.

My mother raised an eyebrow, put the roller in the tray, and wiped up my mess with a rag.

"Why don't you let me do that," she said.

Climbing down, my bones creaked, my muscles burned. My heart fluttered in my chest like a caged bird. I haven't been sleeping and my nerves feel raw. It's the house. It's my father. It's the girl. I can't stop thinking about her. I feel as if she's just out of reach. I wasn't planning on telling my mother anything—she has enough to worry about—but she took the brush from me and wiped paint off my nose and asked if I was okay.

"What do you call remembering things that never happened?" I said.

She wanted details, but the harder I tried, the less I remembered. Plus, with the radio playing some sappy duet and the summer sun shining through the window, the entire thing sounded crazy. The guy across the road was working on his truck. Someone somewhere was grilling hot dogs. There was no place in the normal for it.

I touched my forehead. The bruise has faded to a sickly yellow. I watched my mother paint around the light switch and told her about being in this house with my father, how we lived here without her because in . . . I don't know what to call it, this alternate reality . . . she was the one who was dead. It doesn't make sense, but how else did I know about the broken lamp? The water stain? The stuck window in my room? The flickering light above the bathroom sink?

My mother has an explanation for everything. She'd known about the lamp, too. She'd talked with the movers and the painters and the real estate agent—talked to everyone on her cell phone in the chair beside my bed in the hospital. She thinks I'm remembering bits of conversation that took root while I was unconscious. "Think about how a sound can worm its way into a dream," she said. The bathroom light? The water stain? Maybe the accident dislodged memories I'd recorded during the walk-through. It's how hypnosis works. You see it on TV all the time. People in hypnotic states recalling a license plate number or a tattoo, a key piece of evidence used to crack a case.

"You've been through a lot," my mother said. "We moved and we lost your father. On a stress scale, that's off the charts. Add the accident and your brain injury. It's normal that you should feel strange right now. I feel strange right now."

"You're right," I said. But she's not. This is different. I don't know how to explain. "Parallel universe" isn't right. This isn't science fiction. I've been thinking about it. It keeps me up at night. It's almost as if when you die you go to a rest stop, to refuel or whatever. A layover on the journey between this life and the next. Some kind of cosmic womb, maybe. I know it sounds stupid, but it's like a gestation period. Babies aren't just conceived and then delivered. They have to grow and develop before they're born. Maybe you go through the same process all over again when you die.

And then there's the shadow girl. I don't know how she fits

into all this. She was there, too, in that in-between place. Sad and lonely, just like me. I didn't even bother bringing her up. My mother doesn't have to know everything. I'll keep her inside, a secret wish.

When did my mother go to bed? Why did she leave me on the couch? I woke with some stupid infomercial blaring about some stupid product nobody wants. I pressed mute and listened to the house. The insect like hum of electricity, the pop of floor boards settling, the whine of the fridge turning on. I'd taken a pill at eight, and my body was fused to the cushions. I dragged myself to the kitchen for a piece of fruit, looked in on my father, and went up to my room to wait.

There it is now, the sound I've been praying for. The crackle and hiss of a distant fire. My skin tingles. It's the girl from the In-Between. A voice, hushed and urgent. It rises, lapping at my ears, my nose, my eyes. I'm burning. Her shadow dances across the wall, reaches out to gather me in her arms. My brain tells me I should be scared of this girl, this . . . ghost. I fear a lot of things in this world, but not her. I feel nothing but love in her presence. Who is she? Why me? What is her name? Why can't I remember her name? Her shadow darts out the door. She wants me to follow, but I don't know how. The MP3 player on my nightstand lights up. A song is playing through the earbuds. I hold my breath and listen. It's burned into my brain, carved into my heart, that song—The Last Song.

twenty-three

the girl who lives in the last house before the river is down-stairs on our couch. Autumn Pulaski. She and her mom came by with brownies to welcome us, the new neighbors. Autumn's mother said they baked them this morning, but I'm really hoping that Autumn had nothing to do with it. She's got a nervous condition that makes her pick at her skin: Acne. Freckles. Bug bites. Whatever. She's full of holes. That's mean. She's okay, I guess. I just hate meeting new people. Unless you immediately click with the other person, it's awkward trying to find stuff to talk about. I'm not like my mom. She can talk to anybody.

My mom and Mrs. Pulaski went off to the kitchen for coffee, leaving me in the living room with Autumn. I wasn't really dressed for company. Not that it mattered. Autumn was wearing cutoff sweatpants and one of those wrestler tanks with the over-sized armholes. I plunked down on the couch, trying to look bored with the whole situation. Autumn took it as a cue to plunk down, too.

Me: So, what's there to do around here?
Autumn: Don't eat the brownies. Our cat licked them.
Me: Uh, thanks?

The clock on the bookcase ticked away in slow motion. After five minutes of staring at each other, I decided it would be less painful to stare at the TV instead. I turned it on. The second I put down the channel changer, Autumn snatched it up and flipped to a show about people with bizarre addictions, like eating dryer lint or sleeping with a waffle iron.

"I'm a digger," Autumn announced. "But I'm trying to quit. Do you like air hockey? My mother says I can get a tattoo when I'm sixteen. I heard you were in a car crash."

It caught me off guard, her bringing up the accident. She was the first person to ask about it. I touched my forehead and watched a woman in a commercial sniff her family's laundry.

"I was. I died. But they brought me back to life."

"When I die, I want an open casket," Autumn said. "I'm too pretty for a closed casket."

Is she for real? I wondered. *She's joking, right?*

Autumn was picking at her back. Her armpit was showing. I could see she hadn't shaved today.

"What?" she said, checking her fingernail for blood. "You want a closed casket?"

"I think I'll have one of those brownies," I said and got up and left the room.

I just heard the screen door slap shut. I think they're gone. I know they're gone. Here comes my mother pounding up the stairs. It's not a happy sound.

twenty-four

today when I was carrying some boxes up to the attic, I came across Lucy's cat bed. It was covered in orange-and-white fur. I swept up a little pile with my fingers and put it in a zip-top baggie. I have some of my father's ashes, too, in a small jar with a black metal lid. My mother had already broken the seal on the urn. She'd placed my father's watch inside—the one she'd had engraved for their anniversary. He was wearing it when he died. The crystal was cracked, but it was still ticking, smooth and steady as a heartbeat. Tomorrow we say good-bye. We're burying him in the cemetery in the bigger small town.

twenty-five

My mother's at the dinner table slumped over a glass of wine. This was a lousy day. Actually, lousy doesn't even begin to describe it. What kind of day are you having when the jerk running your father's funeral keeps calling your father Dick? My father is Richard. Sometimes he went by Rich. I get it. People make mistakes. But did he not see the only two people in the cemetery cringe every time he said it? Did he not see the crushed rose in my mother's fist? I wanted to scream at him. I wanted to strangle him with his paisley tie. It was the worst eulogy ever. I couldn't even listen. I focused on the sun glinting off the urn, the leaves shushing in the trees. I was watching a bird peck at a crumbling gravestone when something over by the crypts caught my eye. Under a willow, a stone angel, her hand raised. I thought she waved, but I know that's not right. My brain was playing tricks again.

When the jerk was through butchering my father's memory, he wanted to talk, console us with a few shallow observations about life and death. I turned and stalked back to the car. He should've met with me before the funeral. In five minutes I could've told him a few things about Richard Moss. I would've told him that Richard did not like sports. He didn't cook things on a grill. He wasn't into cars or guns like Scilla's dad. He didn't fish or hunt or drink beer.

My father was sick more than he was well. But when he was well, he loved to read. Anything and everything: books, newspapers, my stupid poems. He loved looking at the stars and telling bad jokes. He loved music, especially jazz. I have some of his albums on my MP3 player. There's one song in particular, by a guy who blows the saddest trumpet ever. Listening to him, you want to die. Not my dad. It had the opposite effect on him. You know how Ritalin is speed, but give it to kids with ADD and it slows them down, makes them normal? This song was like Ritalin. It made him want to live. When he played it, I knew he was on the mend. The darkness was lifting. This is for you, Daddy.

twenty-six

It's happening again. That unnerving feeling that I know things, things impossible for me to know. It makes me dizzy, as if I'm watching everything from far away. I was not in the room in our old house when my mother packed the box she marked MINE. It contained personal stuff, important stuff to her: mementos, keepsakes, souvenirs. I know I sound like a bad magician preparing everybody for a really dumb trick, but it's true. The box was sealed. Today, I sat on my mother's bed and watched her cut the packing tape with a knife. And I knew what was in that box. I just knew.

High school yearbook. A rose from my grandmother's casket. Drawings I'd done as a kid. My mother dropped a small velvet pouch on the dresser. It sounded like buttons. I'm not sure which is creepier: that I knew it was baby teeth or that my mother had saved them. I couldn't breathe. The visions kept coming. Concert tickets. Letters. A stack of photos rubber-banded together. I opened the window, inhaling sharply. The air was warm and smelled electric. A storm was coming. Wind shook the tree out front. Through the leaves I watched a girl in yellow shorts go flying by on a bicycle. Seconds later, the same girl, dressed in pink this time, went flying by again.

I turned to my mother and asked if she'd ever had a miscarriage.

She raised her eyebrows in surprise. I'd caught her off guard. "Why would you ask that?"

"I don't know."

"Did you go through my things?"

Blood rushed to my face. My heartbeat quickened.

"You did, didn't you?"

"I didn't. I swear. It's another one of those things. Like the lamp. Like the water stain."

"I never had a miscarriage," my mother said.

I turned back to the window. The girls—one in pink, one in yellow—were across the road now, straddling their matching bikes. They looked up and waved. The sky rumbled. I closed the window.

"Sometimes you scare me, Elanor."

My mother went back to her box. Digging. Poking. Searching for something.

"Is this what you're talking about?" She handed over two grainy, black-and-white photos on thin, filmy paper. I'd seen them before. I knew them, had held them.

"I was pregnant with twins. That's you. There were two babies, and then one day one of the babies disappeared. It wasn't a miscarriage, though. A miscarriage is different."

"If she didn't come out, where is she?"

My mother let out a sound like a leaky tire, a sound that said, *Can we not do this now?*

Fine. You can learn anything on the Internet. It's called Vanishing Twin Syndrome. It's more common than you'd think, but that doesn't make it any less freaky. My mother was telling the truth. The baby never left her body. It entered mine. "Absorbed" is the word they use. A nice way of saying "consumed," I guess. Devoured. Ingested. It all means the same thing: I'm a cannibal. Like I'm not defective enough.

twenty-seven

On the bed beside me is a plain white envelope. Jackson postmark. Liberty stamp. My name and address in purple ink, in Priscilla's slanty hand. It came while Mom and I were at the mall getting our hair cut and shopping for school. It's after midnight and I still haven't opened it. I'm paralyzed by this crazy fear that it contains something hurtful and mean. A rising dread that makes my fingers tingle. She was my best friend until she wasn't. And then I tried to die. But that didn't change anything. She still treated me like I was something noxious. Like I polluted the privileged air she shared with Natalie Paquin. Priscilla was responsible for The Worst Year of My Life. What could she possibly have to say to me now? I should just open the stupid letter already.

My heart races. It's good. It starts "Dear Ellie" and ends "Your Scilla Monster." She's sorry about my dad. She's sorry about everything. When she heard what happened, she went to the cemetery and sat with my stone angel and cried. Over the summer, she's had time to think. She's changed. *Can we be friends again?*

I should run downstairs and send an e-mail that says I forgive her and love her and maybe she could come stay with me next summer. But I can't. I don't know what's holding me back. I keep rereading her letter. It's short. Scilla never liked to write. In English she always picked the biggest font for her essays. Teachers aren't stupid. She always got marked down for it. What am I waiting for? Maybe it's New Ellie. Maybe it was shopping with Mom. We pretended I was on one of those shows where they make you toss your ugly old clothes and help you pick all new outfits. Miniskirts. Leggings. Silver knee-high boots. (Mom wasn't sure about the boots, but I begged until she gave in.) Fat metal bracelets to hide my scars. The only difference is we don't have a lot of money, so we ended up at one of those fashion discount stores. Everything looks great until you examine it closely and realize it's defective. Like me.

Who am I kidding? I'm not going to waltz into school on Wednesday and suddenly be the kind of girl who everyone is dying to know. I'm not that lucky. That's not how my life works. I'll write her back. I know I will. Just not now. I'm waiting for the In-Between girl. I took one of my mother's pills and my eyelids are heavy. The window is open and I can hear the crickets chirping and the trees sighing. I'll sit here until I hear her coming down the hall. My stone angel. The floorboards will groan. My bedsprings will creak. Beneath the sheets, I'll feel her warmth. My heart glows in her presence. When she's with me, I don't need Priscilla or Autumn or anyone else. What we have is ancient and binding. An eternal pact written in blood. Breaking it would set the monster free.

twenty-eight

When Autumn's not picking at her skin, she's picking at her nail polish. She's doing it now. Sprawled on *my* floor, listening to *my* MP3 player. She gives me the skeeves. I don't know why she can't sleep on the couch. This is all my mother's fault.

Today Mrs. Pulaski invited us down to their place for a cookout. Hamburgers, hotdogs, stuff like that. My mom brought macaroni salad. Their house is big and old and needs more work than ours. There's blue shag carpeting throughout, and avocado walls, and all their furniture is sad and tired, stuff you'd see sitting by the side of the road. I learned some things about their family. Autumn's dad is a deadbeat living in North Carolina, and her brother, Will, is in the military, which explains the ARMY MOM sticker on their station wagon. Their yard is mostly dirt because the river floods every spring, and the chicken coop is empty because wild dogs ate all their hens.

I also learned Autumn's mom works third shift in a factory that makes a million pills an hour, and that her grandma stays with her at night but she's away for the long weekend. Which is how Autumn ended up on my floor. She was going to spend the night alone, in her own house. All Mrs. Pulaski said was, "Can my daughter call you if anything happens?" You know, like the house is burning down, or someone's breaking in.

"She's welcome to stay with us," my mother said.

Autumn looked about ready to pee her shorts. Off she ran to pack a bag. As I watched her go, I saw a girl—my girl, my stone angel—in the tree. Her shape, her shadow, in the bark. She waved. She was leaving. Good-bye. I knew my mother couldn't turn around and uninvite Autumn, but I said, "Make her bring a blanket and pillow. I'm not sharing my bed."

My mother acted all innocent. "Why? What's wrong?"

I rolled my eyes.

My mother made a face. She was ashamed of me. "You've got a bad habit of making snap judgments," she said. "Give her a chance. I think you two have a lot in common."

Translation: She's a reject, too.

Thanks for the vote of confidence, Mom. Just because I'm a reject doesn't mean I want to be friends with one. Making up with Scilla is sounding better and better.

The worst part about Autumn staying over is I won't be able to sleep. No sleep equals no stone angel. No girl from the In-Between. I need her to feel normal. I'm going out of my mind. I'm an addict, cold and edgy, craving that crazy high I get when we're together. I saved my bed for her, but it doesn't matter. Her message was clear: She won't come around with Autumn sprawled on the floor, humming out of tune, her giant feet stinking up the place. I hate her. Make her go away.

twenty-nine

"Are you nervous?"

That was from Mom this morning, up before dawn making me breakfast. Today was the first day of school. My first day of high school. My stomach was in knots, but when she asked, I said no. I didn't want another pep talk.

If we'd stayed in Jackson, I would've had another year of middle school. Here in Pottsville, ninth grade is high school. The school isn't actually in Pottsville. It's in the bigger small town, on a hill surrounded by pines. I have to ride the bus, which blows. In Jackson, I used to walk. Every day with Priscilla—until she turned on me. Then I walked alone, the long way, the roundabout way, to avoid crossing paths.

When I boarded this morning, all eyes were on me—the new girl in the frilly skirt and killer silver boots. It was unnerving at first, but then I saw some smiles and thought, *This is my New*

Beginning. Old Ellie was back in Jackson, a distant memory. Everyone was watching to see where I would sit, but I waited for Autumn to find a spot first. She stalked down the aisle—head lowered, stringy hair in her eyes—clutching her backpack to her ugly cardigan. She was wearing the kind of boots you'd see on a farmer cleaning out a stall. *Keep going,* I thought. *Right out the emergency exit.* When she plunked down in the last row, I thanked God and slid into an empty seat in the middle.

I was digging through my bag, trying to look focused and bored at the same time (a look that always worked for Natalie Paquin), when a girl with swoopy bangs and a toothpaste commercial smile leaned over the seat and said, "Hey, I'm Jess."

"Elanor," I said. "Call me—" Jess shot back like I'd breathed garlic in her face.

My heart sank. Stupid Autumn was hovering in the aisle. Jess made a face like, *You know this loser?* I didn't move. Autumn just stood there. The bus driver hollered, "Pulaski, sit." Jess looked down at Autumn's feet. "Nice boots." She smirked.

It was over before it began. Autumn ruined everything, tainting me with her reject status. They could smell it on me. *Loser.* I wanted to elbow her sharply in the ribs. She rambled on about some stupid thing. But I stuck my earbuds in my ears and pretended she was invisible, staring out the window at the fields. I've done nothing to make Autumn think I'm her friend. Waiting for the bus, I'd barely said two words. She thinks because she slept over we're somehow united, like I'm supposed to be her ally. She couldn't be more wrong. Truthfully, I don't even care about being friends with people like Jess. Girls like her are nothing, zero. Not while I've got my stone angel. She's all that matters. Really. But I want it to be my choice. Me rejecting them, not the other way around.

I'm not going to lie. The rest of the day was a disaster. Nothing played out the way I'd imagined. How stupid am I? Did I really think it was going to be all that different from Jackson Middle? They have rich kids and poor kids and geeks and princesses and jocks and clowns and bullies just like every other stupid school in this stupid country. Compared to Jackson, though, it's small. Really small. The only classes I don't have with Autumn are foreign language—I'm taking French, she's taking Spanish— and gym. Usually I hate assigned seating, but today I was grateful every time a teacher pulled out a chart and told us to get ready to move. It got me away from Autumn. There's not a huge spread between M and P, but there's a Nelson and a Patterson and a Pierce keeping me from stabbing Pulaski with my pencil every time she starts picking.

If only they had assigned seating in the cafeteria.

"You talk in your sleep," Autumn said, sliding her gray plastic tray down the empty lunch table I'd picked by the juice machines. She plunked down across from me and stuffed a fry in her mouth. "Don't you want to know what you were dreaming about?"

I stared at my food-pyramid lunch from home and dreamt that if I ignored her she'd move to another table.

"'Take me with you,'" she said, digging at a scab on her neck. "That's what you said."

"Can you not do that while I'm eating?" I snapped. "It's gross."

The scars on my wrists started itching. I glanced around the cafeteria at the tables filled with normal boys and girls. Boys and girls with friends. Boys and girls joking and flirting and gossiping. I wanted to go sit with them, but walking up to strangers and introducing yourself is awkward. Just thinking about it made my legs shake. It was easier to stay with Autumn.

"Everybody here sucks," Autumn said. "Pottsville sucks. I want to work on a cruise ship."

"Have you ever been on one—a ship?"

"No."

"Then how do you know? Maybe you'll get seasick. Every place is the same. You know that, right? Nothing will change. You'll still be you, even in the middle of the ocean."

Autumn shrugged. "You should come, too. We can share a cabin."

"Let me get my life preserver." I sounded like a complete bitch. I sounded like Natalie Paquin. Sometimes I don't know why I do the things I do. I used to get snotty with my dad when he told his corny jokes in front of Scilla or tried to hold my hand in public. But then a wave of guilt would rush in. He wasn't trying to annoy me; he was just being my dad.

"You're not setting sail tomorrow, are you?" I said.

Autumn shook her head. "No. I meant when we graduate."

"So I've got time to think about it."

Autumn smiled. I rolled my eyes, but in a nice way, the way Scilla used to roll her eyes at me when I'd get on some stupid, crazy kick, like making a movie or learning to levitate. I picked up my trash and tossed it in one of the green bins against the wall. A girl from my French class was standing nearby with Jess from the bus. They were watching me, whispering. "Nice boots," the girl from French—Kylie, I think—said when I passed. I felt myself swell with something like hope. I thought she meant it, but Jess had done the same thing to Autumn so I know she didn't.

None of this ended up in the e-mail to Scilla. In the e-mail, I'm lucky to go to this school. I'm in high school, not middle, which is a totally different experience. There's none of that petty bullshit like we had to deal with at Jackson. All the kids are really nice and want to know all about me. The classes are small and everyone is pretty much friends except for this one girl who everyone hates because she's a total freak, living in her own little world. It was all lies—most of it, anyway—except for the part about Autumn. And the stuff about my new best friend. I called her my stone angel. I couldn't tell Scilla that I don't know her name, this girl . . . this ghost. I made it sound like she's someone I met when I got to Pottsville. "She's way cooler than Natalie," I wrote. "And nicer, too. You'd love her. She's great."

I'm not done with it yet, the e-mail. I want it to be perfect. I saved it as a draft. I don't know why I care. That's not true. I do know, but it kills me to admit it: I miss Scilla with all my heart. We grew up together. My mom and dad treated her like family. Scilla's in almost every memory I have of my life since first grade. It's hard to let go. She was like a sister to me. I know I have my girl from the In-Between, and she should be enough. She is enough. But honestly—if I'm truly honest with myself—I have to wonder if she's not something my damaged brain created, something I made up to get over losing Scilla.

thirty

i came upstairs to write about the shitty thing I did
to Autumn today, but none of that matters now. I
spotted it the second I sat down at my desk: Someone had moved
the ribbon that always marks my last entry in this, the Pegasus
journal. My mother. How could she? Fury boiled up inside me,
and I started shaking.

But as I turned to the page my hands shook harder. It wasn't
my mother. Toward the back of the book, in the middle of a
blank page, scrawled in red ink:

You carry my heart. (You carry my heart in my heart.)

A line from my favorite poem. It is and it isn't. That's not how
it goes, but it's her. The girl from the In-Between. I know her
handwriting. It's burned into my memory. I keep staring at my

palm like it holds the answer. The air is electric. I'm electric. My skin tingles. A current surges through my veins, warming my blood, tickling my cells. I'm not losing my mind. She's not some figment of my bruised brain. She's real. My heart soars. Higher and higher. I'm suddenly whole. A veil has been lifted. I'm aware of everything—the bright scent of turning leaves, the moth-white moon shining over the yard, my mother humming softly to herself in the bathroom.

Below her message I wrote:

Help me find you. What is your name?

I keep checking and checking. Nothing. Not yet. It's not like e-mail, you idiot. An answer isn't going to just magically appear while you're sitting here. I need to stop. I need to go do something.

thirty-one

"Who's Madeline Torus?" my mother asked, gritting her teeth at the computer.

My stomach nose-dived, and my face burned as if I'd been caught stealing her sleeping pills. Worse. As if she'd discovered my father's ashes in the jar in my drawer.

"Priscilla's mother called," she said. "Who's Madeline? You should know. You sent this." My mother turned the monitor so I could see. She crossed her arms and waited.

The e-mail started out fine:

Sweet Darling. My Scilla Monster. You know you meant the world to me.

But then I kept reading. They weren't my words.

Why did I slit my wrists over you? I should have slit your throat instead.

I told Priscilla that she was dead to me now, that Madeline Torus was my life, my universe, a shimmering silver star in an endless black void. I stopped before I got to the end. I couldn't read anymore. My eyes refused to focus. I couldn't concentrate. (Concentrate. Concentrate.)

"Is she someone from school?" my mother hounded. "Did she tell you to write this?"

"I didn't do it."

"Ellie, it's in the sent file. I sure as hell didn't write it."

I swear to God, it wasn't me. I'd saved it as a draft—the e-mail—to work on later. She sent it—Madeline Torus. The girl from the In-Between. Try telling that to my mother. Try telling that to Priscilla.

Mrs. Hodges told my mother that she understands that I've been through a lot, but what I wrote was just plain cruel. I need help. My mother agrees. She thinks I need to see someone—a therapist maybe, or a counselor. Knock yourself out, Mom. Make an appointment. Ground me. Do whatever you want. It doesn't matter. My stone angel has a name. It's Madeline Torus. I'm not insane. She exists.

Correction: existed.

Later, after my mother went to bed, I went on the Internet. I have to find her family. There's a C. Torus in Florida and a Peter Torus in Virginia, but none in New York. It's an uncommon name, not like Moss. There are hundreds of us in every state, all over the country.

How did she die? I remember scars, pure white scars. Was she a suicide? Who is she, this lost soul? Where did she live? When did she live? When did she die?

Madeline Torus.

I repeat her name like a charm or a prayer.

thirty-two

autumn came over begging me to go with her into the woods behind her house.

"Why would I want to go back there?" It's full of gnats and pricker bushes and God knows what else. Deer, I know. Wild dogs, too. The ones that ate her chickens. I hear them at night, howling.

She said she had to show me something. She said I wouldn't regret it. I followed her down the road to her dirt yard, past the picnic table and the empty coop and into the trees, deeper and deeper, until we got to a lopsided little fort. It was sad, really, but Autumn looked so proud. She'd built it herself, she said, out of old doors. Inside, a plywood floor, a couple of beanbag chairs, and a crate. Wrinkly magazines. A plastic cooler with snack cakes and warm soda. She tossed me a can of grape.

"No one else knows about this place," she said. "You can use it whenever you want."

"Thanks," I said, trying to sound honored. "It's nice."

The worse I treat Autumn, the harder she tries to make me her friend. It made me feel bad—for a little while, anyway—for what I did on Thursday, when Autumn was acting really dumb in health class, and I turned to the girls next to me and said, "Is this school too small for Special Ed?" It got a laugh out of Jess, but looking back, it was a pretty crappy thing to say. It's not easy being mean. I don't know how some people do it. It's not for me. I end up feeling like a jerk.

"So what do you do out here?" I said.

"Listen to music. Watch birds. Spy on people. You wouldn't believe how many couples come into the woods to make out."

Autumn pulled a prescription bottle from her sweatshirt. She swallowed a giant orange pill with root beer, then sunk her teeth into a Swiss roll. "Help yourself," she said. "There's brownies, snowballs, and something with peanut butter."

"What's the pill for?"

"It's a fruit chew. Want one?"

I shook my head and plopped down on a beanbag chair and flipped through a magazine.

Autumn picked at something on her chin, rambling about how she thinks there's a Bigfoot living in the woods. She's seen enormous prints, broken branches, mysterious piles of poop.

"My mother says it's a bear. But it's not. I know."

What I said next came out of nowhere. I told her that I'm haunted by a ghost I met when I died. I needed to tell someone and telling Autumn was like telling the birds, the trees, or one of the rocks at the bottom of the river. No one talks to her. No one listens.

Autumn was mute. She sat there with her mouth open, staring dully, her stringy bangs hanging in her eyes. Maybe her fruit chew was kicking in.

"Never mind," I said.

"Are you scared?" Autumn whispered. "You know, there's this guy on TV who fell off a ladder and now he can talk with the dead."

"It's not like that," I said. "It's—" My mouth was open but nothing came out. I wanted to tell her about Madeline, but I couldn't form the words. I tossed the magazine on the floor and looked up at the ceiling. More doors. One of them had a window in it, like a skylight. The blue-white square darkened as something soared overhead. A cloud. A bird. My stone angel.

When one door closes . . .

"This ghost—it's not your dad, is it?" Autumn said.

"No. My dad's gone. This—"

Autumn tilted an ear toward the door—the actual door, not the ceiling. "You hear that?" I did. The sound of branches breaking. We crawled across the floor and waited, and then Autumn poked her head out. Nothing. No Bigfoot. Just some chipmunks and a flash of something bigger. A deer. We watched it for a while and then went back inside.

"Did you keep any of your dad's ashes?" Autumn asked.

A chill trickled down my neck. Had she gone through my desk? I narrowed my eyes. "Why?"

Autumn picked at the hole in her chin. "I don't know. It's something I would do. I'm weird like that. It was dumb question."

It wasn't a dumb question. It was something I might have asked or wondered about. I told her that when I died, he was there—my dad. It was me and him and this girl who's my ghost. I should've just told her about the ashes, too. And Lucy's fur. It's hard keeping so many secrets. But Autumn offered me her sleeve and said, "Don't cry. We don't have to talk about your dad."

"I'm not crying," I said. "There's something in my eye."

A tear crawled down my nose. I *was* crying but I didn't know why. It wasn't my dad. It was something else. It was Autumn. It was me. It was two freaks hanging out in a musty clubhouse drinking warm soda, listening for Bigfoot, discussing creepy souvenirs. Autumn popping fruit chews like they're medicine; me, wanting so badly to tell her how my best friend is a ghost. What's embarrassing is that I think I was actually having fun. Maybe "fun" isn't the right word. I didn't feel like I wanted to be somewhere else. How messed up is that? I'll never be normal. It's not who I am. I've known this forever. Sometimes it just sneaks up on me.

Autumn pulled a crappy old boom box out from under the crate and popped in a CD.

"These guys always cheer me up," she said.

We sat there listening to her music, some ancient rock star singing about painting the world black. Busy streets. Red hearts. Clear blue skies. Everything bright and cheery. I understand darkness. My father was consumed by it. I guess I am, too. Some days it feels like he's been gone forever. Weeks feel like years. Other times, it's still so fresh, my heart stings. It's easy to pretend he's at work or holed up in his study. Dinner is the hardest. We always ate together as a family, the three of us sitting down every night, even when my dad was sick. That's when I feel it. The void. Mom feels it, too. I can tell by the way she rambles the whole time we're eating, barely touching her food so she can keep us from drowning in all that silence. I try not to think about him too much. I know I'm a crummy daughter.

"What kind of tattoo are you going to get?"

Autumn looked shocked that I remembered or cared. Probably both.

"Wings," she said. Her face brightened as she pulled out a

notebook and sat next to me, showing me her sketches. They were pretty amazing. Autumn can draw really well. I told her so and she smiled. "You're a good soul," she said. "Lonely, but good. You can't see it, but you need me."

"What's that supposed to mean?"

Autumn shrugged. "I don't know."

"I don't need you," I said harshly. "I don't need anyone."

To prove my point, I left. Just got up and walked out, slamming the door behind me. I hurried along the path through the woods alone, listening to Autumn calling "sorry" and "wait," not caring about Bigfoot or bears. Pricker bushes tore at my ankles, branches whipped my face. I couldn't get away fast enough. Away from that cruddy little clubhouse. Away from that song about blackness. Away from the stupid, fleeting thought that I should give Autumn a chance, that maybe we were meant to be friends after all.

Where was my stone angel?

Out on the road, the girls—the ones I'd watched from my mother's window—were standing on the bridge over the river. I don't know who they belong to. Somebody's grandkids, I guess. They don't ride the bus. The girls saw me running and thought it was a game. They started running, too, chasing me until I was in the house, in my room. I half expected to hear them pounding up the stairs. I looked out the window to see if they were gone. Standing in our driveway, looking up at the house, the girls were waving their arms, beckoning me to come back. I closed the blinds.

thirty-three

i'm trying to change, but change is hard. It's not like you can flip a switch. I'm not like other girls. We don't connect. I've tried listening to their music, watching their movies, reading their books, but I end up feeling crappy and empty, like I just devoured a bag of those fake onion rings. I have weird tastes. I'm drawn to dark things, depressing things. I don't know why. It's who I am. Like that photographer who OD'd on sleeping pills, the one who took pictures of deformed bodies and creepy twins and retarded kids in Halloween masks. I love her stuff. Maybe it's because when I look at them I see myself and don't feel so alone. I'd give anything to be on the inside instead of outside, always outside looking in.

My mother's solution: Open up. Get involved. People will like me once they get to know me. I can't be afraid to make the first move, so I'm giving it a shot.

There's a club or committee for everything at this school. Pep, French, Robotics, Bowling, Math, Ski, Glee. A million colored sign-up sheets clutter the bulletin board outside the auditorium, and everyone scrambles to get on the popular ones like Yearbook and Prom. I almost joined something called FFA until Kylie told me what it stands for: Future Farmers of America. They sponsor Drive Your Tractor to School Day. Where am I living?

I joined Key Club instead—whatever that is. I think they raise money for sick babies, which is a good thing, I guess. They're planning a car wash, candy sale, and spaghetti dinner. No one noticed me sitting in back until they needed a volunteer to sell quarter-page ads in the talent show program. That's the last thing I want to do—ask complete strangers for money for a club I know nothing about. My mother says I have to put in my time. That's how it works. Maybe next year I can chair a committee or run for president. Yeah, right. People like Jess get to be president. People like Jess get to walk around school with a camera, shooting her friends for the yearbook. Me, I'm doomed to spend the next four years going door-to-door, pestering people to buy over-priced chocolate.

Autumn doesn't belong to anything. If they had a club for jerks, she'd be president. I haven't talked to her since Saturday when she made that stupid comment about me needing her. I've been spending lunch in the library, stalking the stacks for new poets. It's a decent library, with long oak tables and lots of light. Nobody uses it, unless it's for class. The librarian already knows my name. You can't eat in here, but that's okay. It keeps me away from the cafeteria snack rack.

I've been really, really good, and it's starting to show. I've lost almost five pounds. My mother said that's a bag of sugar. She's not eating, either. She's been sick since the weekend. She's got a bug or something. Last night for dinner, she forced down a couple of crackers to settle her stomach before school. She didn't feel like going, but she had to. It's an accelerated program. If she misses even one class, she'll never catch up.

She's got school tonight, too. She won't be home till nine. My mother worries about me being alone, but I don't mind. I'm not really alone. I have Madeline. She's getting stronger. She's no longer just a shadow, the absence of light. Her energy pulses and I can see her forming, the most blindingly beautiful creature. Dark hair. Brilliant blue eyes. Her voice is stronger, too. It used to crackle like dry leaves. Now every word is smooth and silvery. I know when she's coming because I smell her—earthy and metallic—and my legs start shaking and then my hands.

After my mother leaves, I'll do my homework and watch TV and then take a pill so Madeline and I will become one. I've got to be careful about that—the pills. My mother moved them from the medicine cabinet. I wonder if she knows. I had to go through her drawers to find them. I found something else, too: the ultrasounds buried beneath a stack of sweaters. I know I shouldn't have, but I took them and put them with the fur and ashes in my desk. The other night I asked my mother if she'd named my sister. She said she hadn't. The baby vanished before she and my dad had settled on something.

thirty-four

i don't know what possessed me to join cross-country. I'm the most unfit person I know. Actually, I volunteered to be a team assistant. It seemed like something I could do—hold the stopwatch, keep the water bottles filled, stuff like that. I was watching everybody warm up, waiting for someone to tell me my job, when a fat guy with mirrored shades—Coach Buffman—waved me down from the bleachers. Coach Buffman is anything but buff. He must have read my mind because he slapped his gut and said, "Can't exercise a bad diet.

"You here to run?" he said. "Our team's a little short. We need runners."

I watched the girls in one pack, the boys in another, pounding around the track. The girls were all long and sleek, but muscled, too, toned, like the horses we pass on the way to school. Madeline's built like that, not me. Even in their mud-caked sneakers and sweaty tees, they looked clean and pure and healthy, like girls in a skin-care commercial. They were normal girls, pretty girls, not girls with secret scars, girls with ghosts.

"You *are* a runner, right?" he said.

I tried to see his eyes—was he joking?—and said, "No."

"Have you tried?"

When I didn't answer, the coach started clapping at me. He stabbed his finger in the air and sent me out onto the track. "Go," he shouted. "Give it a shot. You can do it."

I felt stupid out there in jeans. I didn't have the right kind of sneakers, the right kind of bra. My feet striking the ground sent shock waves through my shins, my knees, and up into my back. I could feel my thighs bouncing, my chest bouncing, and tensed when the boys came up behind me. I could hear them sucking air into their lungs and forcing it out, as they split like a hive around the beast dragging down the center lane. The girls were next, ponytails swishing, shorts swishing. They made it look so easy, so effortless, like they could go and go forever. Not me. My chest was ready to explode. My shins were on fire. I was sweating and gasping and my legs had started to wobble.

That was only the warm-up.

Madeline kept me going. Jogging backward so she could face me, she smiled and cheered me on. I made it around the track I don't know how many times. More than twice. Maybe three times. I stumbled onto the grass and put my hands on my knees, doubling over. Digging my fist into the flesh above my hip bone, I tried to calm the pain in my side. The air scorched my lungs and my heart pounded so hard I thought it might stop.

"Good job, Moss," the coach shouted. "We'll make a runner out of you yet."

I wanted to laugh, but I couldn't breathe.

After practice, he took me to his lab. It smelled like chemicals and propane. Coach Buffman's the biology teacher. I'll have him next year. He gave me a permission slip for my mother to sign and a pair of cross-country trainers (on loan until my mother can get me my own) and a pep talk straight out of some feel-good-movie locker room scene. Set high goals. Train hard. Don't be afraid of success.

"I forgot to give you the talk on drugs," Coach Buffman said, reaching back to pull a couple of glass jars from the metal cabinet behind his bench. The jars held two miniature pigs floating in cloudy liquid. One looked pretty normal, but the other was missing its face. No eyes. No nose. Just a wrinkly flap of skin where the snout should be.

"This little piggy's mother was pumped full of junk," he said, swirling the jar with the deformed fetus. "This little piggy's mother was clean." He swiveled on his stool and returned the pigs to their shelf. "Got it? Good. See you . . . what d'ya need, Lane?"

"Coach . . ." It was one of the boys from the team. He was drumming his fingers on the door frame, tapping his foot to some imaginary beat. He was long and restless looking, one of those boys who can't stop moving. Standing still was an effort. He saw me and waved and said, "Hey," and then pointed his thumb into the hall and added, "I'll come back."

I don't know if it was the running or the pigs or the fumes, but I felt suddenly dizzy. "I have to go," I said. My heart pounded rapidly again. Madeline heard it and rolled her eyes. I scooped up the sneakers and the permission slip, and the boy flattened himself against the door. His cheeks flamed as I held my breath and scooted by. He raised his hand one more time and said, "Later."

Hugging the sneakers, I ran for my locker and felt strong and light. Behind me Madeline was calling *Slow down!* and *Wait!* I don't know what got into me. I was flying so fast, she couldn't keep up.

thirty-five

i made a huge mistake. My mother had warned me before we moved to Pottsville: Don't draw attention to my scars. Don't flaunt that I tried to kill myself. People might not understand.

She was right.

It went through the school like wildfire. All day long I've felt their eyes on my wrists. Dialing the combination on my locker, raising my hand for a bathroom pass, every time my chunky bracelets clinked, their eyes whispered, *Pathetic. Desperate. Sick in the head.*

I didn't mean to tell her. We were changing after gym. She'd caught me off guard.

"Are those what I think they are?" Jess squinted, leaning in for a better look.

They were the first words she'd said to me since that first day on the bus. I could've said no. I could've said the scars were from the accident. Everybody knows about the crash—it's a small town. They all know my dad died. They all know about my head injury. I thought telling her would make me seem special. Some sad, lonely creature who needs a friend. That's what I thought, standing there in my socks, my bracelets on the changing bench. I lowered my head and waited for her to reach out and take me by the shoulders. The heartbroken girl with the bruised brain.

I looked up. Her eyes widened. She screwed up her mouth in a weird way.

Behind her, Madeline was shaking her head. *Don't cry, Ellie. Not in front of them.*

All around us, girls were borrowing brushes or copying homework, but Jess just stood there, staring. She looked uneasy. Maybe it was Madeline breathing down her neck.

Pull your boots on. Fix your hair. Forget about Jess. Madeline passed me my bracelets. *Put these on and go to class.*

I'm almost through the day. Study hall, cross-country, then home. My old insecurities are rushing back. I should've known better. Pretty girls don't understand. Pretty girls who like pretty pictures and pretty poems and pretty songs. I don't connect with girls like that. Girls like Jess. Girls like Natalie. They're all cut from the same bright and cheery cloth. They don't understand darkness. They've never felt the claustrophobic panic of the world pressing in, sucking the life out of you.

I understand.

I know. I know. It's just that you've never had to sit by and watch other people take for granted what you've only ever dreamed of having: love, friends, a life. It doesn't matter what I do on the outside. I can't change what's inside. I can't change what I love and hate and fear and admire. I'm still a weirdo.

There's something off about me and they know it. I'll never fit in. It makes me sick to think how much time I've wasted trying to be liked, how much time I've wasted worrying about what other people think about me. I don't want to care, but I can't help it. It hurts that people don't like me. It's always there, the longing.

thirty-six

my mother called me a lurker. I heard her in the bathroom, running water, sobbing softly. She's been doing that a lot lately—crying. It scares me. It's not like her. My mother's a rock. For her, there's always a bright side, a silver lining. It's hard to match her enthusiasm. But I wasn't lurking. I knocked because I thought she might be sick. But she wasn't. She was in the tub, taking a bath. Her eyes were red. I watched her fold a wet washcloth and drape it across her forehead.

"You want some aspirin?"

"No, I'm fine. Sit down."

I sat on the toilet lid and breathed in steam through my nose. It smelled like lavender and old people—that minty gel I rub on my calves at night to keep them from cramping. My mother had fixed whatever was wrong with the lights, but it's still too dark in there. She wants to redo the bathroom. Rip out the ugly pink tile, replace the rust-stained sink. Put up one of those vanity light fixtures, the kind that holds four bulbs. Everything is on hold, though, until she finishes school.

"Ellie, do you ever wish you had a sister?"

Shocks of guilt sizzled down my legs. Did she know about the ultrasounds? If she knew about those, then she knew about the fur, the ashes. What about the sleeping pills?

"Yeah. I guess. Not really. Are you okay?"

"I don't feel well," she said.

"Maybe you should see a doctor."

"It'll pass." My mother sank deeper into the tub and splashed water over her shoulders.

"How are your classes going?" I asked, which cheered her up some. I think my interest surprised her. That's pretty sad. Am I that self-centered? Probably. Yesterday, I walked right by the new car parked in the driveway—she'd bought it while I was at school. We talked a little more (mostly about how I came in last at our first cross-country meet), and then she asked me to do a couple of things around the house—unload the dish drainer, take the chicken out of the freezer, stuff like that. I know I haven't been the best daughter. Madeline's the one who deserves the gold star. She dusted and vacuumed while I took out the trash. It's getting colder now, and the days are growing shorter. Someone was burning leaves. Someone else was running a chainsaw. Autumn was out on her bike—a crappy three-speed pocked with rust.

"Hey," she called, coasting up the driveway.

I was tempted to give her the cold shoulder, but I folded my arms and said, "Hey" back.

"Is it true you tried to kill yourself?" she said.

"Where'd you hear that?"

"Everybody knows."

"That's obvious."

Autumn let my jab slide. She leaned her bike against the bushes like she was planning to stay.

"Jess Nolan's a big mouth. Watch what you tell her."

"Thanks for the advice." I turned toward the house.

"No, wait. You want to come over? We've got a fire going in the backyard."

"I can't," I said. "My mom's sick. I don't want to leave her."

That wasn't entirely true. That wasn't why. Is it morbid to ignore the living so you can be alone with the dead? I can't help it. It's a sickness, this longing to be with her twenty-four hours a day. But she makes me feel so alive. Without her my nerves start to deaden and my feet become heavy bricks. Everything is dull and interminable.

Why can't I be normal?

We never did have that chicken for dinner. Mom's stomach was upset, so I ate one of those healthy TV dinners, the kind with brown rice and no dessert. It tasted like the box it came in. Madeline's gone off to where ever it is she goes and now I'm doubting my decision, wondering if it's too late to take Autumn up on her invitation. I know they're still out there. I can smell the smoke . . .

Never mind. Madeline's back. She's sneaking up on me. I hear her giggling softly, nearer and nearer. Her fingers slide along my collarbone, circling me from behind. My brain explodes. My veins dilate, flooding my body with calm and warmth. All my doubts and fears recede, and I am perfect again. Whole. Complete. She completes me.

This is why I do it. This is why I wait for her.

thirty-seven

Maybe I was wrong about everybody here. Maybe they're so starved for new faces they'll take anything they can get. I was wrong about Jess. She doesn't hate me. She doesn't think I'm some suicidal maniac. She offered me a piece of gum during assembly and told me about a place I should get my mother to take me shopping for a homecoming dress. "Don't go to the mall," she said. "Everyone's going there. You don't want to look like everyone else." She showed me a picture of her dress then—royal-blue taffeta with balloon sleeves—and told me not to tell anyone. She wants it to be a surprise. She pulled a magazine out of her bag and said, "Here. It'll give you some ideas. You are going, right?"

I wanted to ask her if you-know-who has a date—the blushing boy from cross-country—but I couldn't because then she'd know I like him. It's next Friday—the dance. I asked Autumn if she's going. "Yeah, right," she said. "Not in a million years." She said Jess was only being nice to me because she wants to win Homecoming Queen, that she's being nice to everybody, hoping to win more votes. Autumn wants me to come to her house instead. She wants to have anti-Homecoming. She said we can sneak some of her mother's wine coolers down to the basement and play air hockey all night.

I think I'll go to the dance.

The place Jess told me about is ninety miles away, but my mother said she'd take me. That's how badly she wants me to go. Plus she wants me to know she appreciates all I've been doing around the house. I feel guilty taking credit. Madeline's the one who cleaned up the yard—front and back. I hate raking leaves. But I had to pretend it was me. And Madeline doesn't mind. She wants to help because she cares about her Ellie.

I *was* all psyched about the dance until my mother had to ruin it by asking if I was going with Jess, or does Jess have a date? Of course Jess has a date. Derek Jordan. He's a junior. She's going with him. Now, I'm worried. What if I go and no one talks to me? I can't expect Jess to hang around with me all night. What if I buy the wrong dress? What if no one asks me to dance?

My mother says I'm too much in my head. "Go," she said. "Be yourself. Have a good time." She makes it sound so easy. Maybe it is. Don't overthink this.

thirty-eight

We're doing a unit on space. Most of the stuff I already know from my dad. He loved stars. My mom got him a telescope one Christmas, and he used to take me out to this field, way out in the middle of nowhere, beyond the city's orange glow. I remember once we stayed out until four in the morning, watching this star cluster called the Pleiades. We got to see Mars, too, rising red on the horizon, and Venus, a cold, lonely disk in a shimmering swath of low-ranking stars. We'd bring blankets and lawn chairs and a thermos of cocoa, and listen to these all-night talk shows on my dad's short-wave radio. I miss those nights of ours, just the two of us, talking and joking and dreaming. I wonder what my mother did with the telescope?

Our assignment is to find out something about our astrological sign: How it got it's name. When it's visible. What are its noble features (whatever that means). I'm a Taurus—the bull. It's the form one of the gods took to rape some princess. I didn't want to write about that. Mr. Dunkley doesn't know my birthday. If I'd been born nine minutes later, I'd be a Gemini, so I did Gemini instead because of the twin thing. It's made up of the stars Castor and Pollux, twin brothers—one mortal, the other immortal.

It wasn't part of the assignment, but I wrote about it anyway—how they were hatched from an egg, and how the immortal brother sometimes appeared as a swan. The twins shared a bond stronger than regular brothers. They did everything together. They were never apart. When the mortal brother was killed and sent to the underworld, the immortal brother begged the gods to keep them together. The gods granted his wish, but with a catch. They couldn't just go to heaven and live happily ever after. That would be too easy. The brothers were sentenced to spend eternity dividing their time between the palace of gods and the suffering dead.

I'm sure the mortal brother thought this was a good deal. But what about the one who could have lived in paradise forever and ever? Was it worth it?

thirty-nine

nobody knows about the vanishing twin thing. Nobody. Some jerk read my journal and drew a picture in the girls' bathroom of a baby eating a baby. This smiling fat thing with pointed teeth and an arm in its mouth. The other baby was just a pile of parts, with its eyes x-ed out. I went in there before lunch, and there it was on the stall, mocking me. Who? Why? What did I ever do to anybody? I squirted a bunch of paper towels with soap and started scrubbing, but it wouldn't come off. My throat began closing, and I could feel my lungs collapsing inward. I dumped my bag on the floor. I couldn't find a marker, but I found a math compass and started gouging at the drawing, scraping the paint down to bare metal. Sweat dripped down my forehead and my hand shook, stinging from where the compass was cutting into it. The spike snapped off. I threw the compass in the trash, tossed my crap in my bag, and rushed to my locker. Where was Madeline when I needed her?

That's when I saw Autumn, heading for the cafeteria. I grabbed her wrist and spun her around. "Did you draw that picture?"

Her brown eyes went wide and deerlike. She was helpless against my grip. "Ow!" she wailed. "What picture?"

"Don't play stupid! That picture on the bathroom wall?"

I could tell by her confused face that she was clueless. It could've been anyone, really. I'm always leaving my bag in class when I go to the bathroom. I leave it on the library table when I'm looking through the stacks. I leave it in the locker room, right on the bench, during gym.

"What's going on, ladies?" the school nurse butted in. She's short and wrinkly and looks kind of like a troll with her pants hiked up to her armpits.

"I don't feel good," I said. "I'm sick." It wasn't hard to fake. I was a sweaty mess. I wanted to throw up.

She touched my forehead. "You feel warm," she said. "Come with me."

My mother came and got me. She made me take a nap. "You don't want to miss Homecoming tonight," she said, tucking me into bed with that frowny face that makes me want to slap her. I'm sorry. It's not my mother's fault. I can't go, but I can't tell her—not after she drove all that way for my dress, spent all that money that we don't really have. I can't go because I'm afraid. What if it's not just one person? What if everyone is in on it? What if I'm being set up, like that girl in that movie who goes to the dance and gets a bucket of blood dumped on her?

After dinner, I stuck my finger down my throat.

So guess where I'm not? The dance started an hour ago. I keep expecting Jess to call, wondering where I am. I don't know why I think that. She doesn't have my number. What is it that makes me think there's always some giant conspiracy to destroy me? I'm

doing it again. Thinking everything everybody does has something to do with me. But Madeline thinks I made the right
decision—not going. I won't regret it. She has a surprise for me,
she said. A big surprise.

forty

ow did I not know? It was there all along. The signs. Her signs. Her messages. Everything makes sense now—a joyful singing kind of sense. What we have is more powerful than friendship, more powerful than love. We were never meant to be apart. That's clear now. My entire life I've been searching, clinging to counterfeits. It was inevitable. On my bed, on my pillow, is the ultrasound with this scratched into it:

MƸ

Two perfect white stars pierce the endless black sky. In the second photo, the heavens shift and we collide. My thoughts unravel. My chest aches. There's a spot over my heart that burns. A million red-hot pins pricking my skin. The collision didn't destroy her. She is alive and she is with me. She vanished before our parents could name her. The universe named her. God named her. Madeline Torus.

Why didn't she tell me sooner? Why did she make me wait? She said I wouldn't have understood. I wouldn't have believed. There had to be a dawning, slow and natural. A journey from darkness to light.

It's a gift, what I have. I'm not alone. I've never been alone. We were together before I was born. We've been together my whole life, but I was too wrapped up in this world to notice. Blinded by sadness and heartbreak, my loneliness was the illusion. I see that now. I probably sound like one of those born-agains trying to describe what it's like to find God. Only God doesn't compare to finding your sister.

forty-one

Saturday was Autumn's birthday. Her mom took us to the pizza place in the strip mall in the bigger small town. It was what you'd expect—hard plastic booths and cheesy murals of ladies picking grapes and loud guys in football jerseys shouting at the TV—but Autumn was dressed for something nicer. She had on this purple peasant blouse and sky-blue scarf and her hair was done up in a twist. The scarf was from her brother, stationed somewhere in the desert. The blouse was from her mom. I hadn't known what to get her, but my mother said it was rude to go without a present, so Madeline went through my jewelry and found a pair of earrings she thinks are ugly. Autumn loved them. She hugged me and modeled them for her mother, who leaned across the garlic knots to fondle the tiny silver stars dripping from her daughter's ears.

"Please don't be mad at me anymore," Autumn said when her

mother went up to the counter for more napkins. "I'm sorry about what I said. In the clubhouse. Sometimes I say dumb things. I know you don't need me. I need you. You're my only friend. You know that, right?"

I glanced at Madeline—perched on the edge of the Foosball table, watching and smiling—and turned back to Autumn. I don't want to be mean to her anymore. Knowing what I know has changed me. This secret I carry makes me feel special, makes me want to be nice to others. I have something they don't: a connection to another world, a world where my best friend is my sister and my sister is not dead because she was never born. It's time to follow my heart, and it is overflowing with sympathy.

I smiled at Autumn and said, "I hope you're having a good birthday."

Autumn hugged me again. She promised to wear my earrings every day. Some people don't need much. Suddenly, everyone around me—their lives, their worries, their hopes and dreams—seem so small and sad and pitiful. I imagine this is what it feels like to be really, really smart or spiritual or talented, when all you can do is shake your head at the ignorant and be kind because they can never know what you know, feel what you feel, do what you do.

forty-two

tonight after dinner, before we cleared the table, my mother said she had something to tell me. I knew it couldn't be good. She'd hardly touched her chicken.

"I'm pregnant," she said.

The clock above the sink ticked. The kitchen faucet dripped. I silently sat there moving peas around my plate. Eventually I managed, "Are you sure?"

My mother said a test confirmed it. She went to the doctor today. "I'm about three months," she said. "It must've happened right before the accident. The baby's due around late April, early May."

"Are you happy?" I asked. A stupid question. Her napkin was shredded and her eyes were filled with fear and sadness. Anger, too, that here she was again, picking up the pieces of our family alone without my dad.

She bobbed her head around, refusing to commit. "I will be," she said. "What about you?"

I shrugged. A baby. Life will be different. Things will change. Another New Beginning. Another Adjustment Period. We're not even out of the one we're in.

"In case you're wondering, we weren't trying." My mother reached across the table and squeezed my hand. "You'll always be my little girl."

I wasn't thinking about that. Right then I was worried about more practical stuff, like how we're going to do this, how we'll manage. My mother has to finish school to get her Realtor's license. She'd said it herself: The life insurance won't last a year.

"I've been going over it," she said. "They say pregnancy is nine months, but it's really more like ten. I'm taking the exam in March. As long as I pass . . ." She rolled her eyes and sighed. "I'm really going to need your support. If this baby is anything like you were, I was sick the whole time."

"I'll try," I said.

"I know." My mother started collecting silverware and stacking plates. "You've been a big help to me since your father died." She put down the pile of dishes and rubbed her belly. "You're the reason I think I can do this. You've really changed."

Not really, I thought. Giving up cheese-filled pretzels doesn't make me a new person. I wish my mother understood that. It's Madeline who does the dishes and folds the laundry and picks up my room. Me, I'm constantly slipping, slacking off.

I don't know who I am, what I want. That's not true. I'm Madeline's sister and I don't want to waste my time with stupid stuff. I dropped out of Key Club. Not officially—I just stopped going to their lame meetings. They were probably going to kick me out anyway. I never sold any ads for that program like I was supposed to. Today I tried to quit cross-country, and I would've done it, too, but Coach Buffman refused to accept my resignation. I'd put it in writing and put it in his mailbox because I was too chicken to tell him face-to-face. It didn't work. He called me out of study hall and read me the riot act.

"What's this?" he said, pinching the letter by its corner, holding it out like a dirty diaper.

I shrugged.

"That's not an answer. Are you dropping out of school? Do you have a potentially fatal heart condition? I didn't think so. You're not quitting. You've got too much potential."

Coach Buffman says I'm a natural. He can't believe how far I've come since that first day of huffing and puffing around the track. I don't know what he's talking about. Our first meet I came in last. The second meet doesn't count—I got lost and never finished the race. Third, fourth, and fifth: second to last. We run three miles just to warm up, then another three miles to train. I'm exhausted all the time.

"I'll pretend I never read this," he said, crumpling my letter in his fist. "I'll see you at practice."

I went, but only because I was afraid he might bad-mouth me to the team, use me as his real-life example of someone who's not willing to work, who gives up too quickly, someone who's afraid of success. Which is such a bullshit line. Why would anyone be afraid of success?

forty-three

i am sick. Throwing-up sick. Hundred-and-three-degree-fever sick. My brain says I need sleep. But my body says I need a pill. The pills are all gone. I took the final one last Wednesday and hid the bottle at the bottom of the trash. My mother will think she lost them, misplaced them somewhere. If she ever asks, I'll play dumb. *What pills? How would I know?*

Maybe I should get dressed and go outside and get the bottle. It's still in the bag in the can by the side of the house. Maybe I can get more. I can tell the pharmacist my mother's sick and needs a refill. I need to sleep. My mind is like a scratched DVD, looping through the same scene again and again and again. We were in world history. The row goes Moss, Nolan, Pulaski. Jess was smiling at her lap, texting with somebody. Autumn tried to throw me a note, but Jess reached up and caught it. What was I supposed to do? Jess hates Autumn, so I'm supposed to hate Autumn, too. I'm stuck in the middle, between the popular girl and the reject. Like Priscilla was, I guess, with me and Natalie Paquin. It should be an easy choice, but it's not. Autumn lives on my road, our mothers are friends. She wears my earrings every day. I don't want to be mean to her anymore. None of this should matter but it does. In the hall I asked Jess to give me back the note. "You really want it?" she said, making a face like I'm some kind of traitor. Now Jess hates me. Nothing ever changes. People don't like me. Why does it feel like I'm always being tested? Why does everything have to be so complicated? Why can't they let me sleep?

I'm sick. My mother's sick. We take turns with the toilet. I said, "Maybe I'm pregnant, too." My mother frowned. "That's not even funny." But it is. I've never even kissed a boy. I've never even held hands with one. I try not to think about it, but I see boys pressing girls up against lockers, I see girls making themselves pretty for boys. I try to be pretty for the boy who can't stand still, the one whose cheeks burn red when he runs. He is long and thin and shy. He nods when he passes me on the course, and my mouth goes dry, I lose my rhythm, and then I have to stop for air. I wish it meant something, but it doesn't. I'm just another runner—one of his teammates—pounding the path through the woods behind the school.

My mother gave me Popsicles and ginger ale and dry toast for dinner. She has school tonight. She wanted to call Autumn's grandma to come stay with me, but I begged her not to. I'm fourteen. I'll be all right. She made the couch up into a bed and put the cordless phone in my lap with instructions to call her if I need anything, anything at all. She stood over me, torn. "Go," I said. "You can't miss class." She rubbed her belly as if it would help her make the right decision. My mother talked all the way to the door. The key turned in the lock. The engine hummed in the drive. The tires crunched gravel and then she was gone.

I wonder what my father thinks about this—the baby, that is. I wouldn't know. He doesn't talk to me. Madeline says it's good. Madeline says she knew. She knows everything and everything happens for a reason. She flips through the coloring book my mother got me from the drugstore and colors until the pages start to wrinkle and curl, until the black crayon is nothing but a stub.

forty-four

I'm putting up walls. At school, I talk to no one. Not even Autumn. I can hear them whispering. They call me Eerie Ellie. They think I am deaf. They stare right through me. I am a ghost, haunting these halls with Madeline. The two of us are invisible. Books fly off the shelves. Things disappear. Madeline can hear their dark thoughts grinding away at their souls. She tells me their secrets. The boy I like likes boys. Kylie is afraid she's pregnant. Jess takes seizure medication to keep from chewing off her tongue with those blindingly white teeth.

After class, in the woods behind the school, we fly. *Faster,* she sings, *Faster.* The girls are gaining on us, the ones with the glistening teeth, hackles raised. They want to gnaw our bones, bury us beneath the leaves where no one will find us.

Down the mountain, through the mud, I run and run. I am

almost down to bone. My eyes are empty sockets. My stomach is hollow. The flesh burns away. Thinner and thinner, till there's nothing left. This body is meaningless. My soul has flown its cage. They have no idea.

The tree outside my window is bare except for one single leaf, brown and desiccated, twisting in the wind.

forty-five

When I got home from school, Mom was at the table, looking like she was about to explode. I thought it was the hormones—she looks like that a lot lately—until she handed me my report card. It had to be a mistake. A glitch in the computer system. They must have me mixed up with someone else. I don't pay attention in class. I barely study. I imagined some honor roll student trying to explain my grades to her parents.

"This is really something!" Mom squealed. She made that tight-lipped frog smile of hers and bulged her eyes. "I knew you had it in you!" She came around the table then and wrapped her arms around me, the hardness of her belly filling the hollow that used to be mine.

My mother the cheerleader. For her this amounts to a touchdown, a home run, a slam dunk. And I had more good news to give her: I was invited to a party. By Kylie from French.

My mother kissed my head and gripped my shoulders and

held me out in front of her for a good, long look. "See, it's not so hard," she said. "Making good grades. Making friends." I wanted to tell her it is hard. Harder than anything. It's hard taking credit you don't deserve.

It helps that I'm sleeping again. Not on my own. Yesterday, I cut lunch and went into the woods and took the back way down the hill into town. It's against school policy for freshmen to leave campus, but I went anyway, past the lot filled with shiny farm equipment and the ancient Victorians on Main, around the corner and past the gas station where the seniors go for subs. Waiting at the crosswalk, fine white flakes started sifting from the sky. The weather here is stupid. It was seventy last week. In the strip mall, I glimpsed my reflection in the plate-glass window of an empty store and thought it was Madeline. I didn't recognize myself. I've changed that much.

I thought it might be illegal to sell sleeping pills to minors, so I went around the store looking for cheap stuff to add, so I wouldn't be embarrassed when they turned me down. I guess I was wrong. The woman behind the register rang everything up and put it in a bag. The candy bar and tissues were a waste. Everything except the pills ended up in the Dumpster out back.

I made it back in time for art. We studied these drawings by this guy, M.C. somebody. There was one slide of these two hands drawing each other and another that was swans forming an infinity symbol. My favorite was of this castle with all these stairs. When you first look at it, all the people on the stairs are going down, down, down. But if you look long enough, you see that they're really going up. It's an illusion, like my life. I can't tell which way I'm going. I thought for sure I was failing my classes. I thought everyone hated me. And then I get my grades. And then I get invited to Kylie's party.

Sometimes I think I'm going crazy.

forty-six

adeline was wrong. The boy I like doesn't like boys. Which makes me happy, even if I am grounded. It's a long story that started with me sitting alone on a couch in Kylie's basement and ended with my mother accusing me of being drunk.

"Am not," I said, fumbling with the stupid new seat belt.

"I can smell you a mile away."

I cupped my hand over my mouth and checked my breath. All I could smell was toothpaste and onion dip. When I got home, I put my pajamas on backward, so maybe I did have too much to drink. It was worth it, though. I didn't need a pill to sleep last night.

Anyone reading this would probably picture one of those high school parties on TV where everybody's packed into some kid's parents' really nice house. Imagine the crush of warm bodies and beer-soaked shirts and random pockets of love and violence.

Hips bumping, fists pumping, music so loud it rattles the china. That's what I was expecting. Certainly not a bunch of blah-looking kids huddled around a kitchen table cluttered with soda cans and chip bags. It's not like I had a point of reference, though. The last party I went to was in third grade, at a pizza arcade. We wore hats. We sang songs. We crawled through a giant hamster tube.

I felt like a dork walking in with my family-size bag of snack mix, but Jess's boyfriend, Derek, jumped up, knocking over his chair to get to me. He grunted like a Neanderthal and pronounced my name like it is two letters long. "L-E," he said, draping his arm across my shoulder. He smelled kind of skunky as he coaxed the bag from my fist and tore it open with his teeth. "I love you. You're the best." Jess started tossing people sodas from a cooler. Somebody named Duggers tried to light a pretzel on fire. A guy in a hunting jacket planted his face in Kylie's chest. Everybody started laughing and falling all over each other, and then they all got up and stumbled outside, leaving me alone in the kitchen.

I wanted to do whatever they were doing out back, on the patio where the dog was chained up. I wanted to smoke what they were smoking, laugh like they were laughing, but I felt stiff and out of place, so I wandered around the house for a while, checking out the bedrooms and the bathroom. The light was on in the basement, so I went down there. The room was wood paneled, with antlers all over the walls—big ones and small ones, a whole head over the couch. There was a plaid recliner and a coffee table and a big-screen TV on one side, and a washer and dryer and a freezer full of meat—I'm guessing deer—on the other.

Who gave me the vodka? That's what my mother wanted to know. I didn't tell her. That's why I'm grounded. His name is

Radford Lane. I know. Don't laugh. Madeline says it sounds like an address. Everybody calls him Rad. He's a sophomore. He's the boy from cross-country, the one who smiles when he passes me in the woods.

"Whatcha doin' down here?" Rad said, swinging from the pole at the base of the stairs.

I shrugged. I didn't tell him I don't have anything in common with these people. I didn't tell him I wanted to go home. He must've seen it on my face.

"Everybody loves you, you know? They think you're cool as shit."

"Yeah, right."

"Really. They're all upstairs saying they're too lame for you. They think you ditched us and walked home. Jess sent me to find you."

Rad's face is all angles and planes. There's nothing soft about him. He juts out all over—hip bones, backbone, elbows, knees. When he runs, he looks like a jackknife folding and unfolding.

"I can't leave," I said. "My house is like ten miles from here."

His laugh reminds me of my dad's: high and warm and light. "I'll let you in on a little secret," he said. "Unless you're wasted, Kylie's parties are boring as hell. You didn't smoke with them, did you? Good. That shit stays in your system. Coach'll kick you off the team. This'll get you kicked off, too." He pulled a small bottle of clear liquid from his jacket. "But I won't tell if you don't," he said, offering me the first sip.

Whoever says vodka has no taste is a liar. It's like drinking hairspray, but it's worth it. After my face stopped seizing, I sat back and let its queasy warmth ripple through my belly and out into my limbs.

"They're all basically good guys up there," Rad said. "Everyone's just nervous around you." He raised his hand. "Wait. Don't take that the wrong way. You're not like the other girls. They're—"

I twisted my bracelet and thought of Madeline. "Normal?"

Rad made a face like I was crazy. I shrugged and took another sip.

We talked cross-country for a while and then we got onto music. I'd like to think it was New Ellie talking, but I know it was the vodka (and that I thought Rad was gay) that kept me from saying anything stupid or out of place. He'd been standing the whole time—hands in pockets, legs crossed—so I scooted over, making room on the couch, and said, "You can sit down if you want. I promise I won't bite. I won't try to kiss you, either."

Rad kicked the coffee table leg like he was testing its sturdiness.

"That's too bad," he said.

"Which one? The biting or the kissing?"

"Both."

He lowered his body next to mine and rubbed his palms on his thighs, and that's when I knew Madeline had been wrong. A current passed between us, a pulling, like magnets just barely touching. He offered me the bottle again, and this time I didn't hesitate—I took a good, long drink. Upstairs, it sounded like some of the boys were wrestling. Someone had let the dog in and it barked and barked until someone put it back out. There was stomping and shouting and laughing, but Rad and I were fixed to the couch. We talked for what seemed like hours and would've kept talking if Duggers hadn't come barreling down the stairs with a fire extinguisher, threatening to put us out. Nothing happened, I swear. I'm still a good girl on the outside, but inside I know what it's like to want someone so badly it hurts. Not like with Madeline. She's my sister. This is different.

forty-seven

i heard it from Autumn first, at the lockers, after homeroom.

"So what's the deal with you and Rad?"

I kept my eyes glued to the Pegasus sticker I'd slapped on my binder the first day of school and tried not to smile. "Nothing." I shrugged. "Why?"

"Something's going on. Everybody's talking about you two."

She's right. They are talking about us. Ellie and Rad. A giddy current trickling through the halls. They're not saying anything bad, nothing gross. Just that we were alone in Kylie's basement for a *really* long time. We'd be so good together, they say. Wouldn't we make a cute couple? That's what Jess thinks. In English, she poked me with her pencil and flashed her toothy smile. "He needs to ask you out." Like I don't already know that. Like I'm not dying inside, hoping Rad knows it, too.

I saw him a lot in the halls today. More than usual. I think it's a good sign, the way his hand shot up over the sea of heads, the way his eyes lingered. Madeline says I shouldn't get attached. There are things I don't understand. I do understand. She's paranoid. She doesn't know everything.

We didn't have practice today. I thought about not getting on the bus and finding Rad and pretending I'd missed it, so I could go to his house and call my mom. I didn't though. Old Ellie would've flooded his locker with notes. Old Ellie would've hounded him for his phone number or just looked him up in the phone book. I would've called his house and begged his mom to tell him I'd called. And if I didn't hear back in five minutes, I would've kept calling until someone took the phone off the hook.

When I got home, I downloaded all his favorite music on my MP3 player and added all the movies he raved about to the DVD queue. I know where he lives. I found his address and mapped it on the Internet and then zoomed in on the satellite view. The photo was taken in summer when the trees were full of leaves and the grass was deep green. It's a big house with three chimneys and a circular drive and an in-ground pool—the only one in town.

Elanor Lane. It has a nice ring to it. Better than Moss. My mother was right about life, about my life: I have so much to live for. Priscilla Hodges. Natalie Paquin. Jackson Middle. It all seems like a lifetime ago. I still have the scars to remind me. But even they're fading.

forty-eight

i want what we share to be perfect and true. Freshly fallen leaves. Clear, crisp mountain air. Darkly scented pines. Instead we get a condom wrapper on the trail, dishwater-gray skies, and Coach's belly jiggling obscenely. Suddenly everything seems grotesque and distorted, like seeing the world in a fun-house mirror. I concentrate on the sun dying beyond the trees and a V of geese honking and flapping.

We're not a couple yet—it's not official—but when Rad passed me in the woods, he turned and smiled, and there was something different, something knowing and sweet. Rad is pure. His heart pumps blood to his cheeks. His knuckles turn blue from the cold. He's not like other boys. Boys like Brent—always pulling at his crotch—or Joel, with his pockmarked cheeks and creepy eyes. I want to slap boys like that, boys who crack up over a condom wrapper on the trail, boys who talk about tapping girls like we're kegs of beer. I can smell them—the raw stench of adrenaline—and it makes me sick. They cut their eyes at me and elbow Rad, and Rad smiles uneasily, and my face burns and I hate them.

Why do they have to desecrate what is good and absolute? I turn away, pretending not to hear, refusing to let them pollute us. It's like we're in color and everything else is in black-and-white. I will not let them cast their dark shadow over us. When Rad passes, I barely resist the urge to take his hand and run with him, faster and faster, away from here, away from the monsters, threatening and spiteful, waiting to devour us.

forty-nine

i'm still grounded but my mother didn't have the heart to hang up on Rad—the first boy ever to call our house. I knew it was coming. He'd found me in the library, slouched behind a skinny book by the poet who locked herself in the garage with the car running. Autumn must've told him where I disappear to everyday. No one else knows where I go, or how I'm good friends with the librarian now. Ms. Merrill thinks I'm smart and loans me books—poetry, mostly—from her personal collection. She's got good taste. Probably because she's young. Just looking at her, you'd never guess she was a librarian. She doesn't act like one. She rides a motorcycle to school. Not some big hulking thing, but one of those streamlined ones that sounds like an angry swarm of insects. She keeps her helmet on her desk, next to the stapler. Sometimes she brings out coffee from the French press she keeps in back, and we sit together and talk about books and writers and stuff.

Rad likes books, too, just not poetry. I told him he's probably never read anything good. I'm not talking about the crap they make you memorize for English, poems about urns and sailors and May mornings. I read him one about dreams festering and exploding, and another one about a guy selling hot dogs in a ghetto, and then he read me some song lyrics, which are like poetry, too, he said.

I know it sounds corny, but that's what we did all night. I read him poems, and we talked about their meaning, and then we talked about Rad, his life, his family. The conversation was pretty one-sided because I didn't want to scare him off. I'm a freak and my life is even freakier. I learned a lot about him, though, that his mom and dad are still married and teach at the college where my mom is taking classes. That he has two older brothers, Tim and Miles. One's engaged and lives in Boston, and the other is a senior. Rad isn't into sports, just cross-country, and he rides a snowmobile, which he promised to take me out on. And he plays piano—there's a keyboard in his room. He was playing a song when my mother got home. I thought she'd have an aneurism when she heard me still on the phone. But she just poked her head in the door and smiled, and whispered, "Not too late, okay?"

I would've talked all night, but Madeline was getting restless, bored. When she started kicking me to get off the phone, I said good-bye. For the first time since the accident, I feel something for someone other than my sister, and I think it scares her. She's afraid I'll break the spell, jinx us in some way. *Don't get attached,* she says. *You're going to get hurt.* But I know she's not thinking of me. She's thinking of—

I'm trying to protect you.

From what?

Everything. The boy. He'll never understand you. Not like I do.

But I think I—

Listen to ME. Your heart is—

Stop looking at my scars. I would never do that. Not again. Not over anyone.

That's not what I mean. You can't understand. You're not ready. Not yet.

fifty

i can spend hours on the phone every night with Rad, but I can't go out with my friends on Halloween. My mother makes no sense. It's my favorite holiday. I love it more than Christmas, more than my birthday.

"I thought this was what you always wanted for me," I said. "Friends, a life . . ."

"Lose the attitude," she said, then shook her head like she was sorry. She's not sorry. She's enjoying this, ruining my shot at happiness.

"I know what teenagers do on Halloween and you're not going. You're in enough trouble with me. I don't need you getting in trouble with the police. End of discussion."

It's all her fault, what I did at the party. She's the one who wanted me to go in the first place. What did she think we were going to do, sit around and play games all night? That's the kind of party Autumn would throw. Kylie's one of the popular girls. This is what they do. This is what my mother wants me to be. She's been telling me my whole life that I need to jump in, take risks, believe in myself and others will believe in me.

"I had a drink. One drink. Why are you acting like it's a federal crime?"

"I said no. Don't ask again."

Everybody's meeting at the Farm Supply lot. They're probably there now, with their shaving cream and eggs and Silly String. Jess and Derek, Kylie and Brent, Duggers and Joel and Rad. This could've been the night, my night. What if Rad was planning to kiss me?

She can just forget about me helping carve the pumpkin. She's down there now, making popcorn, filling the candy bowl for trick-or-treaters. We've had exactly two: the girls from wherever. I think it was them, dressed as fortune-tellers. I doubt we'll get any more, not on this road.

I hate her. I hope some knife-wielding psycho in a hockey mask comes to our door and stabs her a million times.

That's cold.

Why are you siding with her?

Madeline says I'm not being fair. She says my mother's confused right now, torn. She wants me to go with my friends, but she's worried. So much has happened: my father's death, my head injury, the move, college, her pregnancy. She's under a lot of stress right now. She thinks she's doing the right thing, setting boundaries.

Let's go down and help her with the pumpkin.

Nice costume. Very funny. You know my mother's going to blame me—right?—for putting holes in her good sheet.

C'mon.

You go. I'm tired. I've done everything my mother has asked. I'm glad I didn't waste my time coming up with a costume. This is the first year I haven't dressed up. I love Halloween for the free candy and the horror-movie marathons, but more than that, I love it because it's the one day when you get to be whoever you want. Last year I went as a Rocker Chick. The year before that, I was a Hippie. When I was little, I dressed as a Princess three years in a row. My mother couldn't talk me out of it. It's what I wanted to be. This year was hard. I couldn't think of anything. What do you go as when you are who you want to be? This year I went as Elanor Moss. I went as Miss Popularity. Cross-Country All-Star. Honor Roll Student. The Future Mrs. Lane.

Unless you talk to my mother. She thinks I went as a Ghost. I can hear her down there now, freaking out about her stupid sheet.

fifty-one

*t*he doctor heard two heartbeats. They'll do an ultrasound to be sure. This changes everything.

fifty-two

Someone wants to kill me. I don't understand. What did I ever do to anybody? What did I do to deserve a note in my locker that says I must die. ELANOR MUST DIE. That's what was printed on the pink sheet of paper, in a font nobody uses. DejaVu Sans, I think. I'm sure it's the same demented person who drew the picture in the girls' bathroom. It has to be.

Rad said it's a joke. Somebody messing with me. That's all. Don't freak out.

He doesn't know it's not the first time. He doesn't know about the baby eating the baby on the bathroom wall. I didn't tell him because I didn't want to explain what the picture meant, how I knew it was meant for me.

I can't concentrate. I failed a test in math. I kept reading the note over and over under my desk. Why would someone write something like that? I'm nice to everybody. I have friends. No one wanted to kill me when my life sucked. When I wanted to die, no one wanted me dead. I had to try to do it myself. Maybe it's someone like Old Ellie, someone with nothing, someone with no one. I used to hate girls like me—New Ellie—because they had what I wanted: a life.

Don't freak out. How can I not freak out? How can I not take it seriously? Rad's being naive. My fear isn't irrational. Stuff like that goes on all the time. You see it on TV, in the breaking news and in the crawlers:

Bully Poisons Classmate.
Troubled Boy Apprehended in School-Shooting Rampage.
Teen Dies from Knife Wound.

Just because we live in a Podunk town doesn't mean it can't happen here:

Girl Stabbed 17 Times with Pitchfork.
Friend Says, "I'm Pretty Sure She Wanted a Closed Casket."

It never comes out of nowhere. There's always a journal hidden in a closet or the bottom of a book bag. Sometimes it's a drawing of the killer mowing everybody down.

Other times it's a simple note warning the victim that someone's out to get her.

fifty-three

i don't know where I stand with Rad. We talk all
night, every night, but he doesn't act like Derek
acts with Jess, he doesn't act like Brent acts with Kylie. He never
puts his arm around me. He's never tucked his hand in my back
pocket or hooked his thumb through my belt loop or pressed me
up against a locker. I think we're a couple, but I'm not sure. How
can I tell? On TV, it's always the fidgety boy doing the asking.
Maybe that's not how it works in real life. Maybe in real life you
meet at a party and then talk on the phone for hours every night
and then eventually you kiss and then you are going out. Except
we haven't kissed. Not yet. What if tomorrow he decides to stop
calling me and calls another girl. Then what?

He did introduce me to his parents at the last cross-country
meet. I think that counts for something. His father was nice—he
shook my hand—but his mother stood back, her lips curling like

I was some diseased skeeze. That means *she* thinks I'm his girl-friend, right?

Maybe my expectations are too high. I should be happy he's not pressuring me to have sex. I know Jess has, and if she hasn't, she's planning to soon. You can just tell by the way she sits on Derek's lap, the way he pushes the hair from her ear and whispers things that make her slap at him. We're a long way from that. We've never even held hands. We sit together on the bus on the way to meets, and we sit together going home. It's always dark then, and once I tried to touch his leg, but he flinched.

See? I told you.

Told me what?

Never mind.

fifty-four

autumn's been dressing a little nicer lately, like she's starting to care about herself or trying to impress someone. I don't know who she would've been trying to impress today. It was just me and her, in her freezing clubhouse with the plywood floor and the beanbag chairs, trying to stay warm inside a couple of musty old sleeping bags she'd dragged up from the basement. It seemed grungier than last time—the clubhouse—or maybe it was the lack of light. We haven't seen the sun in days. And it smelled bad, too, like the deer that's rotting on the path with an arrow sticking out of its neck.

"You want me to put on some music?" Autumn asked, lighting a tea candle, strong and flowery to help with the darkness and the smell.

I didn't want to listen to music. I wanted to talk. I'm not grounded anymore and I needed someone to listen to me—that's why I was there. Autumn's the only one I trust. Jess has a big mouth, and Kylie tells everything to Jess, and Rad went to visit his brother in Boston. I trust my sister, but she doesn't understand what I'm going through because she's never lived. She keeps telling me there's a plan. Everything that's happening is happening for a reason. But everything that's been happening is keeping me up at night. I can't help it. I worry. That's just me.

I was all ready to spill my guts, but when I looked up Madeline was frowning down through the window in the roof, pinching her nose at the deer smell. My mind went blank. I just sat there shivering and paranoid and sick to my stomach until Autumn lit a cigarette. When did she start smoking? I don't know. I didn't ask. I focused on the red tip glowing in the dark, pretending I was in one of those reality TV confessional booths. The red light meant the camera was rolling. I should say something, anything. I looked up. Madeline's face was pressed to the glass.

"Do you see her?" I said.

Autumn's blank gaze was my answer. She scratched her head like a normal person, and then sat on her hands. I probably sounded crazy, but I don't care. It all came out in a rush: The death threat and how scared I am. My addiction to sleeping pills. All the stuff about Rad and me, like how we haven't kissed. Everything about my dead sister, my ghost.

Once I got started I couldn't stop. My mother would kill me if she knew what I'd told her. There's some stuff you don't talk about, like how your mother is not happy about being pregnant with twins and got tears all over the ultrasound and said she has choices and it's not too late. Conversations like that are called "kitchen talk" in this house, which means what we say doesn't leave the kitchen. I told Autumn anyway, told her how my mother was crying and apologizing, blaming it on the hormones and losing my dad and the stress of school. And then how later she was trying to take it all back—she didn't mean it, she'd been thinking out loud. I should just ignore everything she says for the next five months.

"She won't get rid of them," I said. "But she's probably praying one of them won't make it, that one of the babies will vanish just like the last time. I know it's hard on her, but I've been praying for God not to separate them."

Autumn didn't say anything. She didn't have to. She hiked up her sleeping bag and hopped over, crashing beside me in my beanbag chair. I looked up. A fluffy white blanket covered the window in the roof. It was snowing. Madeline was gone.

"The only thing worse than taking them both is leaving just one. Believe me. I know."

Autumn hugged me, then leaned back and stared at the ceiling. "We have the power to rebuild you," she said. "Bigger. Faster. Stronger." I don't know what that's from, but I like how it sounds. When I looked over, her eyes were watery, too, and suddenly I didn't feel so alone.

It was warm next to Autumn, squashed together in the beanbag chair. I wish I was still there—in our sleeping bags, in the muffled quiet under the snow, with the shadows and the gray. Because even after the candle burned out, the darkness didn't seem so dark.

i'm tired of talking. Everything I say is useless. It won't change anything. I won't be un-suspended no matter how many times I try to explain it. That's what "zero tolerance" means. It means they refuse to consider extenuating circumstances during sentencing. It means there are no accidents. It doesn't matter that you don't know how the knife got in your bag. It means no one cares that you can't sleep or that someone wants to kill you. No drugs. No weapons. End of story.

Until we got home.

"Why, Ellie? Why?" My mother's face was red. Her voice was hoarse from yelling. She wanted answers. What was I thinking, bringing a knife to school?

In my defense, I didn't "bring" the knife to school. It was already there, one of those X-Actos from art class. Why is it legal in one room and not another? They could've suspended me for stealing, I guess. Except I didn't steal it. Madeline must've slipped it into my pencil case, so I'd have something to protect myself if somebody tried to hurt me.

The sleeping pills? That's bullshit. A knife gives them the right to search my bag? It's none of their business. It's like aspirin. But aspirin's on the list of contraband, too. If you have a headache, go see the nurse. My mother is upset because she does not think aspirin and sleeping pills are in the same category. She went up to her bedroom and started rummaging through her drawers, and then I was in deeper trouble. She couldn't find her prescription. "Did you take those, too?" I lied and she knew I was lying. But how was she going to prove it?

At four o'clock the phone started ringing. Everybody wanted to know what happened. Rad called. Jess called. Kylie called. Autumn came to the door. My mother told them all I'm grounded.

"What else aren't you telling me?" she said. "What else are you hiding? Do I need to go through your room?" Everything about her—her tone, her posture, the way her sadness and confusion dragged at her mouth—reeked of defeat. That was what got to me: my mother's disappointment. The way she sat at the table with her head in her hands, trying to understand. Which is never going to happen. Not unless I start at the beginning, with dying and the In-Between, and finding Madeline, finding my sister. I want to tell her but I can't. She'll think I'm crazy. I'd rather have her think I'm a delinquent, so I didn't say anything. I just stood there in front of her, trying not to look angry, until she got up and rubbed her belly. It was time to lay down the law. I'm not going to spend the next week lounging around, watching television. That's not how it works. This isn't a vacation. There are rules. I will talk to no one. I will not leave the house. I will do my schoolwork, and I will work on my attitude.

"It's like being under house arrest."

My mother winked and shot me with her finger. "That's exactly what it's like."

fifty-six

t's exhausting, really—school. Every single day is a performance. It's hard being the girl everyone there knows as Ellie Moss. Because that's not really Ellie. It's a character I invented, a composite of all the girls I've ever wanted to be—the Natalie Paquins, the Jess Nolans. I could win an Academy Award for it. I've got everybody fooled—Jess, Rad, my mother, my teachers—into thinking I'm smart and good and normal. On the inside, I'm still me: Freak. Mistfit. Loser. A girl with scars, a girl with a ghost. No matter how many friends I have, no matter how many people I win over, my fear is that someday it will all come crashing down. It has to. I can't keep this up forever. Madeline says it's inevitable. She's not trying to be mean, but someday everyone will see that I'm a fake. That's why she's helping me get back to my true self. When I'm with her, I get to wear what I want, eat what I want, say whatever comes into my head. I don't have to be constantly censoring, analyzing, worrying that I'm too stupid or lame or weird or ugly. She loves me for me, because I am her sister and we are one.

My mother doesn't understand. This isn't punishment—being suspended, being grounded. It's a break from all the bullshit. It's so easy to get sucked into the distraction of boys and friends and grades and weight that you lose sight of what's important. Madeline is the only thing that matters. How did I forget that? I won't do it again. Stuck here in my room, it's like we're back in the In-Between. The only difference is that my mother is not my father. She won't leave us alone. She hears us and storms in like a commando: "Who are you talking to?! Are you on the phone?!" And then she stands there confused because all she sees is me, so then she yells, "Turn that music down!" or "Sit at your desk!" or anything to show her authority.

At night, after my mother leaves for school, Madeline and I let loose. We crank the stereo and dance around the house and stuff our faces. My mother doesn't keep anything good in the fridge, like frozen pizzas, and no one will deliver way out here, so we improvise with bagels and spaghetti sauce. Monday, for dessert, I baked a cake from scratch. Last night Madeline figured out how to make chocolate pudding. We ate it warm from the pan in front of the television. It helped me sleep. That and the green bottle of nighttime cold medicine. A shot of that and I'm out by eight. I'd sleep all day except my mother starts banging on my door at seven A.M. God, she's a pain. She talks about me being a lurker, but I have absolutely no privacy.

fifty-seven

i spend every minute with you. I've given up everything for you.

I'm not enough. You *always want* more. You're too *attached* to this life.

That's not true.

Prove it.

How?

Madeline exposes her scars. Not the ones on her wrists. The ones over her heart that form our initials, just like on the ultrasound. A vague memory starts to congeal and then is lost. I think I remember. But barely. What I remember is the absence of pain. She wants to do it again, to me. But what about Rad? What if we ever get that far, how will I explain?

You don't have to worry about that.

Why? Never mind. Do it. Just do it.

fifty-eight

thanksgiving's got to be the lamest holiday ever, right up there with Easter and New Year's Day. There's nowhere to go. Nothing's open. There's nothing to do. I hate the parade, but my mom puts it on anyway, even though she's in the kitchen for most of it. I hate the floats. I hate the bands. I hate the corny announcers with their dorky banter, talking about the weather and what they're going to eat for dinner (like anyone cares), and the way they keep building up what's coming next and then cut to commercial right before something I want to see.

I feel like crap. I spent the night in the attic searching for my father's dumb hat, the one that looks like a roast turkey. And my chest hurts, too. It stings like a paper cut, only a million times worse. I should change the bandage again, but I have to hide the bloody gauze at the bottom of the garbage because my mother is that nosy. She's always in my space. She thinks the babies pressing on her bladder give her the right to barge in while I'm in the shower. But this morning I'd just gotten out and was drying off, and I had to jump in the tub and hide behind the curtain. The bandage is a problem because you can see the white square through a T-shirt, so I had to put on a sweatshirt, and it's a thousand degrees in our house with the oven running. I'm drowning in my own sweat.

Technically, my suspension ended today, but since it's a holiday weekend, I'm off until Monday. I'm still grounded, but I got to talk to Autumn when she came to our door because her mother was with her—they needed more sugar for their cranberries. Living in a bubble the last week—without phone, without Internet— you'd think I'd be starved for news, but I'm not. I don't want to know what everyone's thinking, what everyone's saying. I don't care that everybody's taking my side, saying I have a right to protect myself. They're making me out to be some kind of vigilante or something. It's Rad's fault that anybody even knows about the threat. Some girls were talking about me, starting rumors that I was going to try to kill myself again, and Rad went and set everybody straight. Somehow he feels responsible, like if he'd only taken it seriously I wouldn't have stolen the knife and been suspended. So now I'm the rebel, the dark-haired maverick in killer silver boots. But that's not me. I'm not into self-defense. My answer to everything is to curl into a ball and wait for the world to end.

It's just one more layer to put on every day. This costume is getting too heavy.

It was dark by the time dinner was ready. It was weird watching my mom wrestle with the turkey. That was always my dad's job. It was just the two of us, but she made a huge dinner anyway: dressing and two kinds of potatoes and green beans and rutabaga and cranberry sauce and pie. Ever since I can remember, we always went around the table and said what we were thankful for, but this year there's nothing. My mother must've been thinking the same thing because she skipped over that part and said, "Everything looks tasty!" and "Save room for pie!" Then we just started filling our plates, and soon I was filling my stomach, trying to fill the hole that kept getting bigger and bigger even as I ate.

"Slow down," Mom said. "It's not a race." But it was a race, a race to finish before the tears started. I probably would've made it through dinner, but Madeline came in wearing my father's hat, plunking down in the chair that would've been his. For the first time ever, she didn't make me feel better. I felt worse. I could feel it welling up inside. There was something hard in my chest, like I'd swallowed a bone, and then my chin started trembling and everything went blurry. Trying to keep it inside only made it worse. My head filled up and then my lungs. I was drowning. Running upstairs for tissues, I thought, *I should've just stayed dead. We should've all died.*

Looking at my reflection, I hardly recognized the girl with bloodshot eyes staring back. She was vacant and pasty, one of those they rescue from some creep's basement after ten years. You see them on the news, ruined and stringy, standing there stiffly, not knowing how to hug their own mother. I understand how it feels when the familiar is strange and the strange is familiar. I have too many secrets. I don't know how to cope with all this sadness. It sneaks up like a dark shadow, twisting, squeezing the breath out of me.

It's always been my job to help with clean-up, but my mother made me tea and made the couch into a bed like she does when I'm sick. But I'm not sick. Not physically. My heart is broken. Hers, too. I felt bad she had to wash all those dishes alone, but that's how she deals, by doing. She wouldn't let me help. When she was done, she melted into the recliner and put her swollen feet up, checking the channel guide for something good to watch. She breathed deeply through her nose and let it out. She was set-tling in, winding down, and when I looked over I knew by the funny way her eyes were squinched that she was thinking what I was thinking: If my father was here, this was when he'd be bug-ging for a sandwich.

He did it every year, every Thanksgiving, right after Mom and I got everything washed and dried and put away. "Who's ready for a sandwich?" he'd say. And then he'd be up, poking through the fridge, dirtying dishes. Mom and I always groaned and complained. How could he be hungry again? But he was. And every year he'd shout from the kitchen, "Want one? I'll make you one." And every year we'd be like, "Ugh!" and "No way!" and "Don't make a mess!" And then we'd be like, "Yeah . . . okay . . . make me one, too."

Not this year. Tonight, nobody did anything with the left-overs. We never even ate our pie.

I didn't mean all that stuff I wrote in the beginning, about hating Thanksgiving.

I just hate this one.

fifty-nine

3 Easy Steps to a New You!

Step 1—Wake up thinking today is the day you will get him to kiss you. Wear your shortest skirt, your highest heels. Pay special attention to makeup and hair. Wait for him at his locker. Tell him you need to speak to him in private. Arrange a time and place to meet—lunch, say, in the woods behind the school. Spend the next three hours worrying about your breath and chapped lips. Get to the woods early. Apply cherry-flavored balm. Chew a piece of gum. When he arrives, act like you just got there. Pretend you're not freezing and swallow your gum. Get close. Tell him how much you've missed him, and how the last week has been the worst week of your life, and how you never want to go that long without seeing or talking to him again. Let him apologize for not taking the threat against your life seriously. Don't let him go on too long about it, though. Make sure he understands that you do not blame him. Let him know that you know he would never let anyone hurt you.

At this point he may start talking sports, about the meet you missed last week and some guy who broke a school record. Don't be distracted. Get closer. He will go, "What?" and look at you funny, like he's afraid he has dandruff. He will start drumming his fingers on his leg. Tell him you want him to kiss you. If he laughs nervously, wonder if your sister was right and ask him again. Wait for it. It's coming. He may look like he's about to bolt, but he won't. He will pitch forward and grind his mouth against your mouth. His kiss will feel like a fist. Don't pull back, even if it hurts. Especially if it hurts. Notice every detail: his teeth nicking your gums; his tongue like a slug in your mouth; the way your tears slide sideways and tickle your frostbitten ears.

Step 2—Get drunk. If your mother doesn't keep alcohol in the house because she is pregnant, call up the girl down the road and invite yourself over. Make small talk with the grandma while the girl sneaks wine coolers up to her room. The wine coolers will taste better than vodka. They will taste like punch, making is easier to chug one down like water at the end of a race. The girl will gawk in amazement and ask if everything's okay. This is your chance to tell her about your humiliation and pain. Show her your lips, still raw and sore. Tell her your teeth hurt, too. The girl will offer you her wine cooler and say it's not your fault—you are the boy's first real girlfriend. There was Tara somebody in seventh grade, but that doesn't count because it only lasted three days. Say something funny. Come up with a nickname for the boy, Hoover or Lizard. Apoco-Lips. Laughing will make you feel better. Reach for the wine cooler and act surprised that it's gone. If the girl isn't afraid of getting caught, she will go downstairs for more.

While she is away, use the opportunity to reflect on the true meaning of friends. Think about how the girl risking everything to get you another wine cooler meets all of the qualifications. Think about how you should be home, working on your process essay. Wonder if your sister is writing it for you. Stumble around the room, examining the girl's possessions: posters of wizards and dragons; ceramic angels, their hands folded in prayer; a jar of colored rocks; a mirror covered in lipstick kisses. Think about how this girl would do anything to be your best friend. Remember how rejection feels, how it felt being alone. Give in to your sorrow.

When the girl returns, she will see you've been crying. She will hand you a bottle and wipe away your tears. Say: "Sorry." She will laugh, shrug, then stare deeply into your eyes. You won't know how to explain it, this sad but happy feeling. It will start down low in your heart, a burning. Something warm and liquid will flow through your body and you will believe what you are about to do is right.

Step 3—Kiss the girl. It will last less than a heartbeat, but in that instant you will experience something worse than dread. Fear will force you to stumble back, dropping your wine cooler. Watch the red liquid foam pink. Watch it soak into the blue carpet. Curse. Apologize. Repeat. Stand aside while the girl mops it up with a beach towel. When she looks up and says, "It's okay, don't worry about the mess," make your escape. Listen to the girl call, "Don't go!" as you book it down the stairs. Ignore the grandma watching TV. Forget your coat. Run down the middle of the dark and lonely road. The girl will come out waving her arms. She will stand in the road, calling you back. Someone else will be calling you, too: your sister. But your sister seems so far away. Miles and miles away. You have to make a choice. You can't have both.

You are not so drunk that you can't make it home.

sixty

the library is quiet. Too quiet. I have this sickening sense that something bad is about to happen. I don't know how to explain it, this siren wailing in my head. My scars itch—the ones on my wrists, the ones over my heart. There's a nagging in my bones, my gut. Every little thing seems significant: the hush of cellophane as Ms. Merrill loads a cart with books; the soothing gray carpet and artificial trees and endless blond wood. It all sounds so ordinary, right? That's just it. That's how I know something is wrong. Watch an interview with any survivor; they all say the same thing: *It was a day like any other day, nothing special, nothing new.* I can't stop this crushing panic. I should *do* something— run, hide, smash the alarm box and save us all. From what? Earthquake. Fire. A boy with a grudge and a gun.

You should be so lucky.

Madeline wanders over to the stacks, starts randomly pulling books off the shelves. She's acting strange—restless and distant. She wanted to skip school. She had it all worked out. She wanted to spend the day in Autumn's clubhouse, except I didn't have my coat. Autumn brought it to the bus, but by then it was too late. Everyone had seen me. No one's talking about yesterday. Not Autumn. Not Rad. They're probably off comparing notes. I don't know how to explain what happened.

Madeline stalks over, wearing Ms. Merrill's shiny black helmet. It's freezing, but all she's got on is a tank top and leggings. She plunks down next to me, leans back in her chair, and puts her boots on the table. She's got the visor down, so I can't see her eyes. All I see is my own dark reflection staring back. She flaps her fingers for me to give her my journal.

Start with Autumn. Rad, I get. I knew that was coming sooner or later. But Autumn? What the hell was that about?

It wasn't anything. I just wanted to feel *something*.

She's ignoring what I've written. She's drawing a feather on her upper arm with one of Ms. Merrill's permanent markers. It's beautiful. It looks so real.

She leans over the table. My breath steams up the visor.

Why are you wasting your time with all this? You don't have to, you know? You have a choice. It's not too late. It's never too late.

My eye catches something dark crouching by the computers. There's a flash. The pounding of feet on carpet. My heart stops. My brain screams *Run!* but my body goes rigid. This is it. It's over. My life. I'm ready. I'm not ready.

You're ready. We're ready.

Another flash. And another. More feet. More running.

The flashes keep coming, but it's not the end. A voice shouts, "Don't move!" Another voice shouts, "Classic!" It's Jess. Derek is with her, and Kylie, too. Jess with her camera, shooting pictures for the yearbook. They're bearing down, circling me like vultures. Their yellow eyes sharp and glistening. There's no escape.

"You look like a badass," Derek says. He reaches out and flips the visor. Kylie plunks down on the table, beside my boots, and pops her gum. Jess flashes a sinister smile at the preview screen. Her breath smells like death, rotten like the deer carcass in the woods. "Perfect," she hisses. "You're gonna love these."

sixty-one

my fingers contracted. They shriveled and curled, collapsing like a cold, hard star. Madeline crouched on
the bed, on her knees, and put my fist in her lap. Her hands
washed over my hand (tighter, tighter). Her fingers grazed my
knuckles, swept past my wrist, circling back and over, again and
again, until everything around us began to dissolve, until my
heart steadied, and my breathing slowed, and I was there and
nowhere else.

Until the phone rang. It was probably Rad.

Concentrate. Concentrate.

I was trying, but there were a thousand distractions. There
was the cold, hard rain battering the window and the wind howling. The ceiling above my desk was wet, and Rad was calling
(again), and the house shook, creaking and groaning like some
decrepit monster.

Babies crying, people dying. Concentrate. Concentrate. People crying, babies dying.

Headlights swept the wall. The wind caught the storm door. I heard my mother struggling. Madeline opened my fingers slowly, one by one. They unfolded like petals, blooming. My fingers were not my fingers. My hand was not my hand. I closed my eyes, steadying myself.

Stick a knife in your—

"Oh my God!"

I did not open my eyes. It was my mother. It was my mother before the accident, before the RV went through the guardrail and destroyed everything. It was my mother helpless and scared, bracing for the impact. But it was too late. The blood was running down, pooling in the crook of my arm. I heard crying. (Concentrate. Concentrate.) My mother crying, "Oh, God! No, Ellie! No! When did you . . . how long have you . . . when did you start cutting?"

sixty-two

When I got back from my run, our living room looked like the stage on one of those trashy TV talk shows. Mrs. Pulaski was yelling, and my mother was frowning and holding her belly, and Autumn was crying and bleeding.

"What happened?" I asked, wondering why everyone was crying and yelling, why Autumn was bleeding.

"Don't play dumb," Mrs. Pulaski said, poking her finger at my chest. "You know damn well what happened. If you ever touch my daughter again . . ."

Three months ago I might've looked at Autumn standing there a battered mess and made some snide remark about a run-in with Bigfoot. Not anymore. Autumn's my friend. I know I still get embarrassed when Jess sees me talking to her, but I would never hurt Autumn. It wasn't me. There isn't a violent bone in my body. But Autumn swears I did, I swear I didn't, and Autumn's got the bloody nose and bruises to prove it.

"Is this for the other day?" Autumn mumbled into the bloody towel. "For what happened in my room?"

My mother (to me): What happened the other day?
Mrs. Pulaski (to Autumn): What happened in your room?
Autumn (to me): I wasn't going to tell anyone.

I picked at the bandage on my palm.

My mother crossed her hands above her head calling for time-out.

"Calm down," she pleaded. "Let's all calm down. There's got to be some mistake. Autumn, when did this happen? Where?"

"When we got off the bus, Ellie said, 'Let's go to the club-house.' But when we got to the woods, she started whaling on me with her book bag for no reason."

"No, I didn't! I got off the bus and came home. I went up-stairs. I—" I faltered. I don't know what I did. Listened to music, I guess. Started my homework. Then I went for a run. "I didn't do it. Why are you lying? Tell your mother you're *lying*."

Suddenly Mrs. Pulaski's face turned purple and blotchy. I thought she was going to hurt me—shake me or slap me or some-thing. "You're lucky I don't press charges," she growled through clenched teeth. My mother was standing there rubbing her belly like she hoped Mrs. Pulaski might feel sorry for her condition and dial it down a notch. But Mrs. Pulaski was furious. Hers was the kind of rage that makes your pupils huge and your veins pop out, the kind that makes you oblivious to the spit spraying from your mouth.

That's when I tried to leave my body, to reverse time. I was back in the woods, running through the leaves and the snow, the sun through the trees warming my face. Sneakers pounding, blood pounding. My eyes fluttered open. It didn't work. I was in the living room. Mrs. Pulaski was still raving like a lunatic. I couldn't look at her. I couldn't look at Autumn—bruised and sad—mumbling about how she'd tried to outrun me. I stared at my bandage instead, waiting for my mother to step in.

"Elanor, go upstairs," she said, sternly. She meant my room, but I sat on the landing. Not that I really needed to hear what she was about to say. How could she stand there and tell Mrs. Pulaski that I had psychological issues? How could she tell her that this was the last straw and she would make sure I got help, treatment, some kind of therapy, because something was deeply wrong. She actually called me "disturbed." Mrs. Pulaski doesn't care. She said if I ever go near her daughter again, there will be hell to pay. She started to say something about reporting this to the school, but Autumn cut in, stuttering about how her mother didn't understand.

"Ellie didn't mean it. It was her . . . Ellie . . . but it wasn't."

I wanted to storm downstairs and ask, "Which is it, Autumn? You can't have it both ways. I did it or I didn't. Get your facts straight before you go and unleash your mom on me." But I didn't. I went to my room instead. Madeline was waiting stretched out on the bed—ankles crossed, back against the headboard—listening to music through the earbuds. She was wearing a short-sleeved top and adding to the feather she'd drawn the other day. There were at least a dozen now, all different shapes and sizes, trailing down her arm. She smiled and waved, kicking my book bag to the floor. She wanted me to sit, and I wanted to run. But I couldn't move. I stood there in the doorway, my eyes locked on my book bag.

My bag. My bloodstained bag. My bag stained with Autumn's blood.

sixty-three

M-A-D-E-L-I-N-E-T-O-R-U-S. Her name is a death sentence: E-L-A-N-O-R-M-U-S-T-D-I-E.

She's ruining my life, destroying me through me. She's a cancer. Her love is all-consuming, a dark dream of one-and-only devotion. There's no room in our world for anyone else.

Don't you see? They can only tear us apart.

It was all her. The drawing in the bathroom, the death threat, what happened to Autumn. Everything. She's using my body against me. She's using me to destroy my world, a world where she doesn't belong. Trying to lure me with this: a silver sliver hidden in my journal. The tool of my annihilation. An invitation to return to the perfect void we shared in the beginning.

Yes. No. You don't understand. There's a plan. You're complicating the plan.

I try to speak, but she swallows my words. I'm choking. I can't breathe. I love her. I can't live without her, but I don't want to die. She's in my blood. I have to release her. I have to get her out.

sixty-four

You carry my heart. (You carry my heart in my heart.)

Help me find you. What is your name?

part iii
the true north journal

*Nobody can go back and start a new beginning, but
anyone can start today and make a new ending.*
—Maria Robinson

sixty-five

i hate doctors. They act like they care, but they don't. You're nothing but a machine to them, something to fix. The one who glued me together smelled like rotten cabbage and wore brown clogs. He measured out kindness with a dropper. The psych ward doctor is worse, with her frizzy mad-scientist hair and that clipboard of hers. She squints at me over her reading glasses like she's examining a germ through a micro-scope. She interrogates me with stupid questions: Do I hear a voice? Does the voice tell me to do things, warn me of danger? Do I feel fingers touching me?

I answered her truthfully. I told her about Madeline. I told her my sister is living inside me, and she bobbed her head know-ingly, like she's seen my kind before. She's got a label for every-thing: Depression. Bipolar Disorder. Early Onset Schizophrenia. (Translation: nut job.) I'm seething with the same rage I felt the day we buried my father, when the funeral director kept calling him by the wrong name. I want to scream when she calls me those things. I want to hit her over the head with her stupid little clipboard when she looks at me that way. She's labeling it everything but what it is: possession. She promises to make me well. She thinks she's so smart, but she doesn't understand. I did not want to die. I did what I did to keep living. I don't blame anyone for jumping to conclusions. I know how it looked: a girl with suicidal tendencies admitted to the hospital with multiple lacerations. I look like the victim in a slasher movie. Like that time with my hair—I started cutting and couldn't stop.

I need a priest or a medium. I don't need a psychiatrist. I don't need pills with names I can't pronounce. Drugs won't drive her out. I can't see her or hear her, but she's not gone. Not really. She's just been closed off. It's like we're in prison, in adjoining cells in solitary confinement. I can hear her tapping on the wall . . .

The only one I don't hate here is Erika, but Erika's not a doctor. Not a real one, anyway. She's a therapist, which means she smiles a lot, even though her teeth aren't that great. She's better than the woman back in Jackson, the one I had to see after I tried to kill myself. She was into hugging, that one, like it was the answer to all life's problems. She gave me the creeps. Erika's not like that. She smiles, but she keeps her arms to herself. We meet in a room with a couple of plastic chairs and some inspirational posters and not much else. For an hour a day she acts like she really cares about what I have to say. I don't know. Maybe she does. Maybe she doesn't. She gave me this journal. It's got a soft cover, like a spiral notebook, but with a ton of pages, like maybe she thinks all that blank space will distract her patients from offing themselves.

I have to trust her. I have to make her understand what's going on. I've come clean about everything, all my secrets: the In-Between, the initials over my heart, my addiction to sleeping pills, what happened with Autumn. We talk about other things, too, like my father and mother, and how I feel about the babies and school and Rad, and the healing process. We talk about love and betrayal and death and loneliness. I talk until I can't stand the sound of my own voice, until my throat hurts and it's time to shuffle back to my room. After we meet, I feel good for a little while but not for long, because that's when I start to feel Madeline pacing back and forth like a caged animal. Her silence scares me. That's when I realize I could talk to Erika forever and take my pills and still never be whole because how can I be complete when Madeline is my other half?

sixty-six

my mother is not the most subtle person. It's pretty obvious she's hidden everything with an edge. All I wanted was to remove the stupid hospital bracelet before I took a shower, but I couldn't find the scissors or the nail clippers. Apparently, I'm not even allowed to shave my legs—my hot-pink razor is missing. On the bathroom sink is a purple tube of hair removal cream.

Something else is different, too. My room. She's been through it, I can tell. Evidence of pine-scented cleaner. No trace of blood. Everything's a little neater. My clothes are hung, and my socks are paired, and my comforter smells like fabric softener. I checked my desk drawer. Lucy's fur, my father's ashes, the ultrasound of me and Madeline—they're all gone. They're probably with the scissors and knives. That's fine. I understand it has to be this way. She's probably read my journal, too, the old one, the one with the Pegasus on it. I don't care. She knows everything already. It feels good to be rid of all those secrets.

My mother's been productive. She collected my missed assignments and weatherized the windows. She even pieced together her favorite lamp, the one I broke in the In-Between. All that while I was off "getting well." It's a joke, really. It sounds like I had an infection, something curable. The doctor said maybe my breakdown was the result of the accident or genetics or a chemical imbalance. Whatever. I'm still a head case. Nobody wants to visit a head case. If I'd been hospitalized for a normal reason—like pneumonia, or I had my appendix out—I'm pretty sure someone would've come to see me. Don't you think my room would've been filled with friends and flowers and balloons? But nobody came. Not one person. I was there for three days.

"You weren't allowed visitors," my mother explained. "Only family."

"Did anyone try?"

"Autumn did," my mother said. "Autumn tried."

Autumn? Really? Autumn wanted to see me? What about Rad? What about Jess and Kylie? Ms. Merrill? Coach Buffman?

My mother hesitated, uneasy with where the conversation was heading. Erika had given her the talk about "triggers," and how she needs to avoid them for a while, at least until my meds stabilize. She's walking on eggshells, treating me the way she used to treat my father. She's tiptoeing around the truth: Everyone is afraid of me.

"Don't worry," I said as I shrugged and frowned and shrugged again. I told her I don't care. It doesn't matter. I would have been embarrassed to be seen like that: drugged up and cut to pieces. My mother even had a hard time looking at me. I know she doesn't believe me. She thinks I'm upset, but I'm not. It's the drugs. They make you feel this way, like the world could come crashing down around you and all you'd care about is what's for dinner. The last time the doctors tried to fix me, my father refused to let them put me on anything. He said it wasn't healthy. My mother disagreed. They fought about it—a lot. I remember my mother shouting, "God, Richard! Do you want her to end up like you?"

There are things I should be doing—homework, calling Autumn, calling Rad—but I can't peel myself off the couch. Not today. Talking is an effort. I'm tired from my shower, and my cuts sting from the soap. I'm suddenly aware of gravity, the air itself weighing me down. I feel like a rock at the bottom of a river. Correction: not a river. A river is clean and alive and follows a course. I'm stuck at the bottom of something thick and stagnant, a bog or a swamp, something choked with rot. I am the evil ogre on the couch, hiding beneath blankets, waiting to reach out and snap your bones. The only comfort is the newfound quiet in my head, silence for the first time in four months.

sixty-seven

erika's office at True North is a little nicer than that ugly room at the hospital, but not by much. It's clean and bright and new, but you can tell in five years the veneer will start to peel. The walls will get grimy and the fake leather chairs will crack and come apart at the seams.

"So," Erika began, "how's it going? Did you finish that book? Did you like it?"

This is how all our sessions start. We talk about normal things for a while—TV, my new nail polish, music—and then we get down to business, the real reason why I am there. Erika sits up a little straighter and crosses her legs so she'll have something to write on, and I have to remind myself I am not her friend and this is a mental health center and she doesn't really care about all that other stuff.

Today she asked about Madeline.

"Do you think there's a reason why your sister waited fourteen years before making her presence known?" Erika asked. "What I mean is, why did she wait so long?"

"She's been with me my whole life," I said. "She just couldn't ever make a connection. It was the accident that let her do it. I died, you know. I was pronounced dead. I guess my dying opened a door or something."

Erika nodded and wrote something on her pad. She was silent for a moment, and then she wanted to know how I felt around Madeline. How I felt about myself when I was with her.

On the wall behind Erika's chair is a framed picture of a girl in a field with this huge golden bird rising up before her. It looks like an eagle, or a hawk, but much, much bigger, and there are flames trailing from its wings. Erika told me it's a phoenix, a mythical bird that symbolizes immortality. Every thousand years, at the end of its life cycle, the bird builds a nest, and then the bird and the nest burst into flames, and then a new bird—but really the same bird—rises from the ashes.

Staring at the bird, I shrugged and said, "I don't know. Whole, I guess. Complete. We're total opposites—she's everything I'm not—but she loves me for me. I feel . . . we're so close. I've never felt that close to anyone. It feels good not being alone."

Erika nodded. "Do you think all sisters are that close?"

I shrugged. "Twins, yeah." I shrugged again.

Erika read from her pad: "You said the accident opened a door—that's what let you and your sister connect." She tugged at her earlobe absently. "Do you think Madeline turned the accident into a positive experience for you?"

"Yeah . . . I guess?"

"Do you think Madeline has helped you deal with losing your father?"

There's not much to look at in her office, so I end up looking at Erika, at her leather flats and khaki pants and plain white dress shirt. She's not beautiful, but she's got the potential to be cute. With a new hairstyle and a tube of tooth whitener . . . I know I'm not perfect, either, I'm just saying.

"Do you spend a lot of time thinking about your father?"

I picked at the hole in my jeans and told her truthfully that I don't. I don't spend a lot of time thinking about my father. I think about him sometimes, but not all the time. Not as much as I should.

"Do you think about him when you're alone?"

"I'm hardly ever alone. I have Madeline."

"So you're never really alone with your own thoughts?"

"No."

"Tell me about your life before the accident."

I dug my fingernails into the fake leather, leaving sickle-shaped gouges. I waited for Erika to ask me to stop, but she didn't, so I said, "It obviously sucked. I tried to kill myself."

"Did you ever think about suicide when you were with Madeline?"

I shook my head. "No. Never. I wanted to live forever."

"What's it like now, without her?"

I didn't answer because Madeline's not gone. They've given me drugs to build a wall, but I can still feel her fuming on the other side. Unless what I'm feeling isn't really her. I've thought about that a lot lately. Part of me is afraid what I'm feeling are ghost pains, like what Scilla's dad used to feel after he got his arm chewed off in the machine at work. Part of me is afraid if I look too closely, I'll see that all I'm left with is a raw, ugly stump. My sister existed. No one can deny that. I've got the ultrasound to prove it. But then my thoughts sway. If Madeline wasn't real, if I created her, then what does that make me? If I can't believe in her, what's left?

"Ellie? Tell me about Madeline's weaknesses. What are her faults?"

Erika's voice seemed far away. There was a rushing in my ears as the edges of the room turned gray and blurry. Gripping my knees, I closed my eyes and said, "She doesn't have any."

"Is there anyone in your life, besides Madeline, who's perfect? No? What does that mean?"

She wanted me to say that Madeline can't be real because everyone is flawed. I wouldn't do it. I refused. I explained to her (how many times do I have to explain?) that Madeline was never born, that imperfections are the result of living. Living corrupts us. The world makes us impure.

She tried a different approach: "If Madeline is perfect, then why did you say she was trying to destroy you? When we first met, you said that you cut yourself to release her. Something made you think that you needed to put some distance between you and your sister. What happened?"

I know what she's doing. She's trying to drive a wedge between us. Just like Natalie Paquin did with me and Scilla. Every session, she'll just keep hammering away until we split. Madeline wasn't trying to destroy me. I made a mistake. I see that now. She wanted us to be together forever, just the two of us. And I can't fault her for being possessive. I'm the same way. I'm the clingiest person I know.

"She had a plan for us, but I ruined everything," I said.

"Did the plan involve suicide, Ellie?"

The watch on her wrist ticked away the minutes.

"Okay, instead can we talk about your friend Priscilla and how she made you feel?"

I won't let her wear me down. I may be crazy, but I'm not stupid. I know where this leads. I know that someday—maybe not today, but someday—I'm supposed to have this big epiphany. I'm supposed to realize that my sister is actually my subconscious. I created her to fill the hole in my heart. I created her so I could feel special and loved. I created her so I wouldn't have to think about my father or Scilla, so I wouldn't have to go through this miserable life alone.

Sometimes I'm so exhausted I just want to give Erika what she wants. Other times I want to tell her how stupid and narrow-minded she's being. But I don't. I can't. I know that someday I will find proof, and Erika will have her eyes blasted open so wide she'll never be able to shut them again. She will see the truth and she will know.

"Ellie? You said Madeline had a plan. What was the plan?"

I didn't tell her that I don't know—Madeline never told me.

I pointed to her watch instead. We were out of time.

sixty-eight

my wounds are healing. My heart is healing. My body radiates a warm and peaceful glow. I am surrounded by friends offering sympathy and support. Rad drapes his arm protectively around my shoulder and squeezes tight. There are tears and hugs, lots and lots of hugs, with everyone going *I'm here for you* and *You're not alone* and *You could've come to me*.

After Erika taught me about positive thinking, that's what I pictured. That's not what played out. Thanks, Erika. You're a big help. Nobody wants to talk to me. They act like I'm carrying the plague. At the lockers this morning, Kylie croaked, "Hi," then hugged her books and backed slowly down the hall, distancing herself like I'm some scary, stray dog. Jess, she acts like I'm invisible. Every time I see her, she's on her phone pretending to text. Even Ms. Merrill is different. She gave me a stack of books about hope and love and people overcoming their problems.

I guess it's easier if they don't notice, if they carry on like I don't exist. Rad's not even here. He's home sick. Pinkeye, I heard. Everybody else is being nice, really, really nice. But a timid kind of nice. Wide-eyed and cautious, people I don't even know try to get a glimpse. They flinch when they see the scars—puckered skin, rust-colored scabs—like they feel the razor slicing their own precious flesh.

It's Wednesday, so I only have to make it through two more days. My mother wanted to keep me home the rest of the week, but Erika said the longer I wait the harder it will be to go back. She warned me today would be difficult. In every way I'm back to where I started. It's Jackson Middle all over again. I'm like one of those idiots who wins the lottery and ends up broke a year later.

No one wants me here. I can tell. My teachers look at me as if to say, *We're not trained to deal with students like you. We can't teach with you in the room.* I know, because Mr. Dunkley, who never ever gives bathroom passes, was more than happy to see me leave.

I brought this with me—my True North journal. I'm supposed to write down everything I feel today so Erika and I can talk about it later. But when I got to the bathroom I didn't have a pen. Instead I stared at my deformed face in the mirror and wanted to cry, but nothing happened. I couldn't remember how, which sounds stupid. It's like forgetting how to walk up the stairs or how to use a spoon. It's strange. My brain tells me what I should be feeling. *You should be angry,* my brain says. *You should be sad.* But my body seizes up like a machine without oil.

When the bell rang, I was wondering if I should go to the nurse and ask to go home. But classes were changing now, and the door hushed open, letting in all the noise from the hall. "Are you okay?" a soft voice asked. It was Autumn. She was clutching my book bag. The new one, not the old one. My mother couldn't get Autumn's blood out of the old one.

"No, I'm not. And you shouldn't be talking to me."

She came over to the sink and watched me wash my hands and offered me a paper towel. A pack of tenth graders came in to use the mirrors. Autumn caught them gawking and glared.

"You still want to be friends?" I said. "Even if I'm crazy? Even after I beat the snot out of you?"

"I don't think you're crazy. I believe you," she said. "The stuff about—"

She looked around. She didn't want to say it, not in front of the girls whispering nervously behind their hands. The girls checking their eyeliner and hair, giving me plenty of space. Normal girls. Girls who are afraid of the monster in oversized sunglasses and dark tights. Girls who think, *If she could do that to herself, what would she do to me?*

I'm supposed to be in French right now, but instead I'm lurking in the shadows where I belong, in a dark stairwell that goes down to a door with a yellow EMERGENCY SHELTER sign. The bell just rang again. *Slam! Slam! Slam!* That's the sound of doors closing. I can almost hear Madam Bisson breathe a sigh of relief as she notices my empty desk. I'll bet she doesn't even report me. I'll bet no one would say anything if I never came back.

sixty-nine

oday Erika tried to convince me that I'm deserving of happiness. The way she said it made me sound like I'm an anorexic denying myself food. It sounds really stupid, but I kind of get what she means. One time in English we talked about how the mind can make a heaven of hell or a hell of heaven. There are people who have it all, get everything handed to them, and still they bitch about how everything sucks. I guess that's how Erika sees me. For an hour every day she's forced to listen to a girl who was really doing well, really turning her life around, and then threw it all away. For what? An imaginary sister. A ghost. She wants to help me get it all back, rebuild my life. But what if that life wasn't really mine to live?

"What would be a home run for Ellie? What makes you happy?" Erika trotted out her biggest smile so I'd know what a face is supposed to look like when it's happy. She wanted me to copy her example. I tried, but it didn't feel right. Too many teeth were showing. I closed my mouth. Madeline makes me happy, but I can't tell that to Erika. She thinks we're making progress. I told her I want friends and a boyfriend and good looks and good grades.

"Remember what we talked about yesterday? You have all those things."

Correction: had. Not anymore. Jess and Kylie keep their distance. I haven't talked to Rad in almost a week. My jeans are too tight, and my hair looks dirty because I accidentally washed it with conditioner. Cross-country is over, and I missed the banquet. I missed the stupid talent show, too. Erika thinks I'm just being paranoid. It always comes back to fear—fear of succeeding, fear of failing, fear of living, fear of dying. My assignment is to reach out to one person. She thinks I'll be surprised by the results. She thinks my real friends are just giving me space, waiting for me to make the first move, waiting for me to invite them back into my life.

Tell that to Rad. I called him when I got home, but he wasn't there, so I called him again from Autumn's. That's where I go now while my mother is at school. I can't be left alone. I can't be trusted. I don't know how, but my mother convinced Mrs. Pulaski that I'm not evil anymore. What happened to Autumn will never happen again because I'm on medication and seeing a therapist. I'm getting better. I can't blame Mrs. Pulaski for getting angry that day. She had every right. Autumn was messed up pretty bad. I guess Mrs. Pulaski feels sorry for my mother—everything I've put her through, everything she's been through with losing my dad and all—because she lets me stay at her house at night until my mother gets home. Not that Mrs. Pulaski has to babysit. She's at work. It's Autumn's grandma who watches me. She's okay, except we're not allowed up in Autumn's room. We have to stay downstairs with her, so she can keep an eye on us. We do our homework on the couch while Autumn's grandma watches game shows or celebrity news. It's not so bad, really. My mother is there by nine to pick me up.

Tonight she made us spaghetti sandwiches and took us to the dollar store. Autumn was happy about dinner. I guess it's her favorite. It sounds gross, but they were actually pretty good. The dollar store was a bonus, a home run for Autumn. Her grandma needed wrapping paper and bows, and Autumn got to spend the ten bucks she got for shoveling the driveway. We had fun on the way over. Her grandma drives one of those big luxury cars old people drive, with heated seats and power everything. Autumn made up a game where we punched each other every time her grandma hit the brakes for no reason, which was a lot.

The dollar store is the shiniest store in town. It is bright and clean and all the workers wear green smocks. Autumn grabbed a basket on the way in and went down every single aisle, touching and smelling and holding things up for my approval. One of the workers—a fat woman with a knee brace—followed us around with a push broom like she thought we were going to steal something until Autumn pulled out her prescription bottle and offered her a fruit chew.

We were there for over an hour, and then Autumn's grandma found us over in Personal Care sniffing deodorant, and told us to hurry up because it was starting to snow. By the time we got outside, the car was already covered. The headlights shone on big fat flakes sifting down like confetti. Her grandma put on an oldies station so she could concentrate, and Autumn went through her bag of stuff. Hair clips and body wash and another one of those angel figurines for her room. I'd bought some stuff, too, but I kept everything in the bag, afraid that what I bought would break because everything they sell there is cheap made-in-China crap that doesn't last. The whole way home, Autumn kept bumping me with her shoulder, going, "Isn't this great? Isn't this fun?" And that's when I realized Autumn is one of those "heaven of hell" types. She's perfectly content with her crappy little life. Spaghetti sandwiches and dollar store shopping sprees and riding in her grandma's car with her best friend—all those things make her unbelievably happy. A stupid kind of happy. A happiness I've only ever felt with Madeline, when it was just the two of us, alone in the In-Between. Sometimes I wish I could trade places with Autumn, just to see what it's like, if her happiness is real or not. I want to learn to make a heaven of hell because this world is hell without my sister.

When I got home, I tried Rad again, but his mother said he was in bed. I pictured her at a kitchen counter, in her bathrobe and slippers, making faces at Rad's dad, mouthing *It's her, again. The crazy girl who cuts herself.* I asked Mrs. Lane if she thought Rad would be back at school tomorrow. She sighed before saying "maybe," then told me not to call their house so late.

seventy

jess is having a Christmas party next weekend. I'm not invited. I'm sure she thinks I care, but I don't. We have zero in common. I'm nothing but a cheap knockoff of girls like her. I still haven't talked to Rad. He was out again today, and he doesn't return my phone calls. Erika's an idiot. All her advice is useless. In some ways it's not so bad. This is what I'm used to. It's like finding a ratty old T-shirt you thought your mom had tossed. It's soft and familiar and smells like you.

seventy-one

Rad's back. I wouldn't have even known except he came into the nurse's office to get his eyedrops while I was there getting my pill. He acted surprised to see me and said, "Hi." I said "Hi" back and then waited for him in the hall, where he acted all surprised again, like he hadn't just seen me two seconds ago. He raised his pass—he needed to get back to chemistry—but I put up my hand. "Wait," I begged. "Please. I need to talk to you. Just for a minute."

He was wearing a flannel shirt I like and faded jeans and those beat-up sneakers that have covered hundreds of miles. He could've outrun the crazy girl who loves him, but he followed me to the commons where we were alone.

I sat down first, which was a mistake. Rad didn't sit next to me. He sat on the opposite bench, hunched and fidgety, his elbows awkwardly on his knees. I wanted to touch him like I owned him. It was Old Ellie all over again. Needy and pathetic. I reached out, but he leaned back.

"I don't want to give you this," he said, pointing to his eyes, still raw and crusty with infection. He smiled halfheartedly and looked around. He was checking out my scars, but trying to act like he wasn't. I used to do the same thing with Scilla's dad. It's hard not to stare.

"Sorry I haven't called," he said, before rambling about how busy he's been and why he hasn't been in touch. Busy with school and work. "Yeah, work. I got a part-time job." That's why he didn't visit me in the hospital. He had training. A few more apologies and then he was standing.

"Well . . . I gotta run." He said, "I'll see you around. Okay? Cool."

Not *Give me a call, Ellie,* or *I've missed you, Ellie,* or *You want to meet me after school?* No. He looked down and tipped his head and said, "You're gonna be okay, right?"

And I thought: *This is it. He's leaving me.*

I guess I should've expected it. Everyone leaves me eventually. Scilla. My dad. Lucy Cat. Madeline. Now Rad, my first boyfriend.

(Was he ever really my boyfriend?)

I could see it on his face, sadness and fear and worry. He didn't know how to do it. It was the kiss all over again. He was afraid I'd be crushed and try to kill myself. I can see why. I'm a mess. Not inside, though. My insides are gone. I'm a deep, dark void. I can't feel anything, not anymore. I used to be either hot or cold. Now I'm just lukewarm. The drugs leave me flat. Rad was quitting a husk, some shriveled-up dead thing. A mummy. Maybe if I'd cried and begged for a second chance. Who knows? That's not what I did. I told him to wait. I stood up and looked into his raw, pink eyes. I had one question for him, I said. One question before he walked away and never talked to me again:

"Are you gay?"

Rad slumped back as if I'd knocked the wind out of him. He looked shocked and hurt, like I was an evil monster exposing his secret. With all my scars I looked like one.

"Is that what you think?"

"I understand," I said. "Really, I do." My voice in my ears sounded slow and stupid, like I was drunk, like it was the party at Kylie's where we first got together. Except it wasn't the beginning, it was the end. From now on it's all endings.

"You should leave now," he said. "Don't make me say something I'll regret."

My face hardened. My heart was even harder. I moved closer. Someone had to feel something.

"You are, aren't you? That's why you don't like me."

"God, Ellie!" He stomped his foot. He threw his head back. "Don't be stupid! I'm not gay!"

I leaned in for a good-bye kiss, but he blocked my mouth with his hand.

"I'm not gay," he said. "You're just not who I thought you were. I'm sorry."

And now he's gone and I'm alone. Again.

I should go back to class, but I can't move. I want to hate Rad, but I can't do that, either. It's my own fault, for pretending I was something I'm not: normal. Madeline warned me. She said that someday everyone would see that I'm a fake. She warned me about Rad, too. I should've listened. She was right. Not about Rad liking boys. She lied to protect me, to keep me from getting hurt. I'm too broken for someone like Rad. He likes girls, just not this one.

seventy-two

Christmas without my father. In some ways it's not the first. He was always physically there, drinking coffee, opening presents. Mentally? Not so much. This morning Mom and I stuck to the routine. I woke her up, and she made a pot of coffee, and then I waited in the kitchen while she plugged in the lights and put on some music and hung my stocking. She called me in when everything was ready. I found her standing by the tree, pointing to a pile of presents she hadn't wrapped, looking like *Where did these come from?* I'm not totally inconsiderate. I got her presents, too. I guess she was surprised because my dad always took me shopping before his winter blues kicked in.

I gave her one of hers first. It was my school picture, which she'd completely forgotten about, and I had, too, until I found the envelope of prints in the bottom of my locker. The frame I got at the dollar store. There was other stuff, too—oranges from the FFA fruit sale at school, a travel mug, a bag of those gross licorice candies she loves—but the portrait was her favorite. She sat on the end of the couch in her robe, my picture in her lap, sipping her coffee, and looking pleased. It's a good shot of me. No dark circles under my eyes. No cuts. I look normal. I am thin and healthy and happy. The funny thing is, I don't remember that day. What was I thinking as I posed in front of the backdrop with the too-green trees and too-blue sky? Had I just been invited to Kylie's party? Was I thinking about the boy on cross-country who always turned and smiled?

Or was I thinking about Madeline?

My big present was a cell phone. One of the really nice ones I'd been begging for, but now there's no one to text. Unless Autumn got a phone, too—which I doubt. The portrait I gave my mother, that girl doesn't exist anymore. She doesn't know I don't have any friends. Not that I ever had any. Jess and Kylie, they never knew me. Not the real me. The me Madeline knows. The me I guess Autumn knows, too. There's so much I can't tell my mother. I can't tell her Rad and I are over. I want to, but I know she'll just say something dumb and cliché, like *You're young* or *You'll meet other boys* or *There are plenty of fish in the sea*. Not telling her today seemed smart because I don't want to hate my mother on Christmas, especially this one.

"This is so cool," I said, smiling my fake smile. It's the only one I've got anymore.

My mother sighed suddenly, putting down her coffee and the picture. "Let's have some breakfast and get dressed and get out of here."

"What about the ham?" I asked. For the last two days, that's all she's talked about. *What size ham? What time should we start the ham? What should we have with the ham?* I don't know if she didn't want a repeat of Thanksgiving, but she said, "Forget the ham. We'll eat out."

It sounded like a good idea, but the nearest city is pretty dinky. The storefronts were all dark and the streets empty and the gold garland strung between the light poles sagged sadly. I watched the dirty snowbanks go by and felt like I was in one of those end-of-the-world movies. The sky was a gray lid over everything, and I started to wish we'd stayed home and eaten our stupid ham. I could've pretended to text my friends, and Mom could've pretended that the portrait on top of the TV was her real daughter, not some imposter who got her hopes up and then let her down.

We could've turned back—it wasn't too late—but my mother kept driving.

"Where are we going?" I said.

"Does it matter?"

It didn't matter, not to me, but it was weird. It isn't like my mother to do anything without a plan. We kept going—past the car dealerships with giant flapping flags, and the big-box hardware stores, and a run-down motel with a pink VACANCY sign flashing—until we came to a bridge with blue highway signs. My mother put on the blinker and followed the arrows.

"We've got to find gas," she said. She nodded at the phone in my lap. "That thing's got GPS. Figure out where we are, what's next."

I pressed a button and the screen lit up. I tapped a compass and the phone found us and put us on a map. We were the red arrow crawling through the mountains. The view was all wrong for what I wanted. I could only see where we were at that exact moment. I couldn't get it to show me what was ahead. I kept tapping and then the top of the screen went white. We were heading into the abyss.

"I think we just drove off the road."

"I'm pretty sure we didn't. Let me see."

"It's not me. It keeps losing the connection." I showed her the screen.

"Don't worry. We'll find something. Watch for signs."

She looked back to the road, turning the radio up and then down again before looking back to me. "You know . . . I was thinking," she said. "I'm off for a few weeks. If you wanted to have some friends over . . . you could have Rad over . . . he's never been to the house."

I shrugged. "Maybe . . . thanks."

"How about a sleepover? You can have Jess and Kylie. Whoever. Just not too big, okay?"

I didn't want to talk about my friends because they aren't my friends anymore, so I said, "You know, next year's gonna be really different . . . Christmas, I mean. The babies will be—" I counted May through December on my fingers. "Eight months old."

"What do you think they are?" my mom said, glancing down. "Boys? Girls? One of each?"

"Girls. Definitely girls."

"Me, too."

We passed a cell tower so I checked my phone again but there was still no signal, so I stared out the window and watched my breath fog the glass. There was nothing out there, nothing to see, just woods and farms and some low, boxy-looking factories in the distance. Everything was gray and black and white and brown. Muted.

"Ellie? Can I ask you something?"

I shrugged.

"Is the medication helping?"

I shrugged again. "I guess. She's gone, if that's what you mean."

"Do you—"

"Can we not talk about it?"

My mother stiffened. She was making that frowny face she makes when I hurt her feelings. Why did she have to bring that up today? On Christmas? My mother checked the mirrors and gripped the wheel, stepping hard on the gas. We were in the center lane, with a tractor trailer on one side and another speeding toward us from the on-ramp. My body went rigid. The car rocked. Sandwiched between the trucks, I counted the seconds and watched the wheels and waited for someone to swerve. After they passed, I added, "It's just that I feel stupid—talking about her—if you don't think she's real."

My mother's eyes skated between me and the road. "I wish you didn't feel that way."

"I wish you believed me."

Our wishes lingered in the air until I pointed to a billboard for a truck stop.

"Five miles." My mother checked the gas gauge. "We can make it."

The plan was to stop for gas—just gas, but maybe some chips and sodas, too—but the truck stop was new and bright and huge, with a place to do laundry, showers, a video arcade, and even a place to rent movies. There was a restaurant, too. The entrance was just past the drink machines and the racks of sunglasses, and there was a sign that said PLEASE SEAT YOURSELF. We were just looking, but a woman in a Christmas sweater came out, and suddenly we were in a booth by the window, with menus in our hands.

"Is this okay?" my mom asked.

I nodded. "This is good. This is perfect."

My mother scanned the menu and said we needed to start

back soon because she didn't want to be driving in the dark on unfamiliar roads. This place might be the only thing open, and we hadn't eaten since breakfast. I think that's what she said anyway. I wasn't really listening.

I was watching everybody in the restaurant, thinking I should write a poem. I haven't written one in a really long time. It can be like the one Ms. Merrill loves, about breakfast in a bowling alley. But different. Better. I didn't have any paper, so I memorized every detail: the fake Christmas tree by the empty salad bar and the stockings taped to the bakery case and the windows frosted with spray-on snow. I'm going to write about the waitress with the yellow uniform and hot-pink nails who brought us water and silverware and said the pot roast was dry. Then there was the horseshoe counter and the guy with a do-rag eating strawberry shortcake and the guy in camouflage talking on a cell phone. And the people sitting alone in booths: an old lady in a gown looking like she'd come from a ballroom dance competition; a gross guy in a sweatshirt that said I'M NOT SANTA (BUT YOU CAN SIT ON MY LAP); the other waitress—the one with hair extensions—doing scratch-off tickets with a key. I want to write about my mom and me, too: me, looking like I'd gone bobbing for apples in a bucket of glass; my mother in her stretchy jeans looking like she'd swallowed a planet. It's going to be about all these people with nowhere to go, settling for any old place just so they won't be home alone missing a wife or an ex-boyfriend or a husband or a kid or a dad.

Mom got the turkey, I got a hamburger, and we both got pie for dessert. The food was okay, but the food didn't matter. This will be one of those Christmases we'll talk about, one of the ones we'll remember. All the other years will blur together in their sameness, but this one will stick out. It would've stuck out anyway as the first Christmas without my dad. But there are going to be a lot of those for a while: firsts without Dad. We let my father have Thanksgiving. Christmas is ours.

When we were leaving it was snowing. I told my mother about the poem I wanted to write. She smiled and said I should write it, she'd like to read it, and started the car. As we pulled away, I could see the people in the restaurant: our waitress clearing our table, the guys at the counter drinking coffee, the lady in the gown reading a newspaper. And then the scene slid from view and we were back on the highway. I reclined the seat and thought about how all those people back there would have to drive home alone. We had each other, Mom and me. Everything was good in the car, with the heat blasting and the radio playing. Better than good. It was snowing, and my mother had to lean forward to see, but I wasn't scared. For the first time in a long time I didn't feel the weight of everything pressing down. I'd forgotten about Rad and my used-to-be friends and my father and even Madeline. I think my mother was forgetting, too. I think she'd forgotten about my father for a little while and about school and money and the house and my mental problems. It was just the two of us, and the babies inside her, and the future stretched out before us like the dark and snowy highway. We can't see it, but we have to believe it's there.

In the end, it's always about believing.

seventy-three

As soon as my mom stopped worrying about her classes for two seconds, she started worrying about the babies. Specifically: where she's going to put them. Upstairs, there's only my room and hers. Downstairs, there's the computer room, the room that was going to be my father's study. My mother kept saying there's room in hers for now, for the bassinets. "But eventually—"

"They can have my room," I said. "I'll move downstairs."

My mother looked relieved. I knew that's what she'd been thinking but was too afraid to ask. She doesn't know that I hate my room now. It's not the same without Madeline. I can't stand to be in there alone. It's a reminder of everything I've lost.

As soon as it was out of my mouth, my mother was making plans. "We'll keep the Nacho Cheese and Chips. Babies like bright colors. What about your room? It's kind of dark back there. We can do this today, if you're ready. Get it out of the way. We're gonna need help. You want to call Rad?"

I called Autumn. We put the computer on a stand in the living room, and brought some boxes up to the attic, and got my father's desk out to the garage. While my mother was out picking up a pizza, we got everything from my old room moved down. Desk. Bed. Dresser. My books and posters and Pegasus collection, everything except my nightstand and dollhouse. They don't fit in the new room.

The new room is weird, stuck on the back of the house like it is, off the hall off the kitchen. Plus, there are no windows. It's like a prison cell but without the toilet. There's no bathroom downstairs, either, which means I have to go upstairs, and the only closet is in the hall.

"This isn't gonna work." My mother was leaning against the door, her arms folded over her belly, making that frowny face of hers. "I'm sorry, Ellie. I thought this room was bigger."

"It's fine," I said.

"Are you sure?"

My mother wants so hard for me to be happy. Sometimes I have to give her something.

"It's only temporary, right?"

The room is long and narrow. I can sit on my bed and look through my dresser. My desk doubles as a nightstand. My old room was big enough for two, but now I am one. I don't need all that space. At night, buried beneath the covers, with the lights out, the room is warm and dark. Dark as a coffin. Dark as a womb. I imagine this is what it's like for the twins, snug inside my mother, floating in all that darkness.

seventy-four

She's real. My mother sees that now. She has two daughters, not just one. There is me and there is Madeline. She knows I did not invent her. She can't deny it any longer. Maybe Madeline is responsible for what happened. Maybe she called up the storm, knowing where it would lead. It wasn't predicted—all that wind. It came out of nowhere, tearing at the house, huge and powerful, trying to force its way in. I was in my new room downstairs when a sound like the world ending sent me flying upstairs, searching for my mother. I found her in my old room, in the dark, her face pressed to the window. I flipped the light switch but the power was out. Our tree had come down—the one out front—ripping through the lines, collapsing against the house.

I want to jump ahead, but I can't. I have to slow down. Tell it like it happened. I want Erika to read this, so it has to make sense. There was nothing to do at three in the morning, in the dark, with the rain pounding and the wind howling, nothing to do until the storm stopped and the sun came up. My mother wouldn't learn about Madeline for another fourteen hours. A lot had to happen first. We had to call the power company and the insurance company. We had to find the camera. We had to talk to the neighbors who came by to point and gawk and wag their heads at the damage. We had to run to the gas station for coffee and donuts. We had to stand outside, in the cold and the snow, taking pictures of the tree. We had to wait for the insurance guy to show up, and the power guys, and the tree guys. We had to eat our lunch in a dark kitchen, shouting over the chainsaws and wood chipper. We had to go back out and take more pictures of the mangled roof after the tree was down.

Later—after the power was on, and the tree was a pile of logs, and the donuts were gone—my mother and I sat on the couch and went through the pictures. Our heads bent together over the dinky screen, we relived today and the last five months in reverse. There was a picture of the Christmas tree taken before Christmas, and a picture of our Thanksgiving turkey, and one of me on the couch looking like a slob in sweatpants in front of the TV. Mom pressed the button, and there was me crossing a finish line, and me standing with Coach Buffman, and me dressed up for Kylie's party. First day of school. My new haircut. An "after" picture of my mom's bedroom, followed by one of me on the ladder, with paint on my nose.

Mom laughed. I pressed the button.

My father's urn, on the desk, in the room that is now my bedroom.

My mother sighed. I was about to shut off the camera, but I pressed the arrow once more.

"Who's that?" she said.

I couldn't breathe. I felt like I'd been hit in the chest with a wrecking ball. The room started spinning. I was floating. There, on the camera, was the picture I'd taken in my room. But not exactly. It was my room in the In-Between. It was the picture I'd taken of Madeline before I knew my father was dead and my mother was alive. Before I knew my best friend was my sister. My stone angel. She was down on all fours, crawling toward the camera.

"Is that you?"

"It's her!" I cried.

My mother squinted and then snatched the camera from me. "That's you," she said defiantly.

"It can't be!" I snatched the camera back. "Look!" I pressed the reverse arrow. There was a picture of Mom and me packing up our old house. I pressed the forward button. Madeline. I pressed it again. My father's urn. Our camera's too cheap for a time stamp, but it can't be me in the picture. My mother tried to say that she must have taken it right after we got to Pottsville, but she knows it's not true. I had a giant bruise on my forehead. I was ten pounds heavier. My hair was still ragged. I didn't even own that shirt then, not until we went school shopping, and that was after we buried my dad. She knows all of these things. She knows that's not me.

She took the camera again, to get a closer look.

"We're not identical," I said. "Just our hair and eyes. She's beautiful, isn't she?"

My mother let the camera slip from her hands. She stood up suddenly and went to the kitchen and then upstairs. She came back down and asked for the camera and then went back up.

I think she's in shock. I have to give her time. Tomorrow, my mother will call my doctor and she'll call Erika, and I'll show the picture to Autumn, and everyone will know that I am not crazy.

seventy-five

i hate her. I want to scream her to pieces. I want to claw and kick and grind her into oblivion. I can't see straight. I can't breathe. It's tearing me apart. I am splitting. She deleted her daughter, my sister. Erased all trace that she exists. She will be sorry. She will regret this day. Someday. Trust me. She will pay and pay and pay. I knew something was wrong when she tried to make me take my pills. I told her I didn't need them. She told me to take them.

"Why?"

"Don't argue," she said. "Take them and get dressed. You've got a session with Erika."

"You're gonna tell her, right? You're gonna tell her about Madeline."

My mother placed the pills on the kitchen table.

"I took that picture," she said, taking down a glass for juice. "It was you in that picture."

I walked to the sink and tossed the pills down the drain and ran the faucet.

"Where's the camera?"

"Ellie, listen to me. You've changed, but it was you."

"Where's the camera?"

"I took that picture. I must have. A lot was happening then. We just don't remember. Ellie, listen. Please. If she's real, then why did the pills make her go away?"

"It's just—It's—It's—" I started twitching, my muscles contracting grotesquely. My right arm shot out, knocking the glass to the floor. My leg flew back and kicked the cupboard door. It was Madeline's energy—angry—needing a way out.

My mother gripped my arm. "What's wrong? Are you okay?"

I wrenched my arm free. I needed to find the camera.

I lurched up the stairs and down the hall, like some possessed marionette, knocking pictures off walls. I heard my mother on the stairs—she's getting heavy and slow—and heard her calling, "Wait." I kept going. There it was, on her dresser. My hands were shaking. I couldn't stop trembling. I started mashing buttons randomly. Arrow. Reverse arrow. Christmas. Thanksgiving. Cross-country. Kylie's party. School. My father's urn.

The floorboards creaked. My mother was in the hall. She was saying, "Listen to yourself, Ellie. Listen to what you're asking me to believe."

I pressed the arrow on the left. My mother and me packing up our old house. I pressed the arrow on the right. The urn. Left. My mother and me. Right. Urn. Left. Us. Right. Left. Right. Left. I panicked. It was the same feeling I'd had in the Poconos when my father said, *Hold on! We're gonna hit—*

"You stupid—"

My mother slapped me, hard, across the face. Her eyes were wide with fright.

My arm hitched like it was ejecting from its socket. The camera went flying. The stupid piece of plastic crap shattered against the closet door. The shuddering in my chest stopped. I walked past my mother and down the stairs and out the door and waited in the car. The girls were watching, dressed in snow-suits, staring at me from across the street. They waved. I gave them the finger.

It was wrong, what she did, deleting the picture. Even Erika said so. I could hear the two of them, behind the office door, talking like they thought I couldn't hear.

"She's lying!" I shouted from my chair in the hall. Erika opened the door. "Come in, Ellie. Please."

"You're lying," I said. "You believed it yesterday."

My mother's face burned red.

"You know you did. Say it. Just say it."

My mother turned to Erika. "It was a strange picture. It was out of focus. Ellie's changed so much since summer. It caught me off guard."

"It wasn't out of focus. You're lying. You're just saying that now. Here. In front of Erika."

"Ellie, why would your mother lie?"

I folded my arms over my chest and fell into the fake leather chair. I tried to be a stone, a rock, but it started again, in my neck, the flinching. I pulled my limbs in tight, fighting against my own body. My leg kicked forward like a reflex test. Again and again, knocking against the coffee table, knocking Erika's mug to the floor.

"That started this morning," my mother said.

Erika nodded, grabbed a bunch of tissues and cleaned up the

coffee. "It's a side effect," she said. "Her doctor may need to adjust her meds. Ellie, have you been feeling anxious again?"

My head started ringing. Everything melted and my eyes went out of focus. I pinched my lips together and shut my eyes and forced the burning tears down my throat. *I can't live like this anymore*, I thought. *I don't want to live like this.*

"Ellie, answer her." It was my mother. I could hear the embarrassment in her voice, the disappointment. I disappoint her time after time after time. *I don't care,* I thought. *I can't answer.* I won't answer. I'm never talking again. Words are useless. They look at me and all they see is this red, angry, crazy girl, when really I'm dying inside. Can't they see they're killing me? Can't they see I'm dying?

seventy-six

My mother came home with a cat. A scrawny little black thing. That's what I call her: Thing. My mother calls her Sweet Pea, the name they gave her at the shelter. I don't want her guilt offering. She can take it back. She can put it out in the woods and let the dogs have at it. No. I don't mean that. That's cruel. This cat did nothing to me. It's my mother I hate. My mother I'll never forgive. Not ever. She thinks a cat will make up for betraying me, for treating me like I'm crazy when she knows in her heart I am not.

seventy-seven

answer Erika's questions, do what my mother asks, what my teachers ask, like a zombie slave. I don't control my life. They do. The pills do. Every day is wrapped in a blanket of sameness. I am Old Ellie again. Fat. Stupid. Lonely. I go to school and watch Jess and Kylie and Rad, watch the drama of their lives as if I'm watching TV. I listen in on their conversations. Kylie thinks she's in love with Duggers. Jess bought a new purse. Rad and the guys went snowmobiling Saturday night and got pizza. Today everybody's talking about some ski trip coming up. This one's bringing vodka. That one's bringing something else. It promises to be the best. I smile like a fool and say, "I have pills. Lots and lots of pills." But no one hears me. I'm worse than The Reject. That's Autumn's part. I'm worse than Autumn. The Reject has a part to play. People notice The Reject. I'm not even in the show. Before when they looked at me, their eyes said, *How sad. How pathetic.* Now their eyes register zero. I'm the invisible audience.

I switch off the show that is their lives and turn to the Autumn channel. In Autumn's show, I'm the comatose friend. Squeeze once for yes, twice for no. When my mom is at school, I sit on Autumn's couch and write poems in my head, poems that don't make any sense when I put them down on paper. They're just random words. Things I pick up from TV or conversations between Autumn and her grandma. Things like: *There's more here in the small than there is in the big.* When I'm home, I sit on our couch, with Thing in my lap, and watch TV and eat all the foods that used to be off-limits. Tonight I ate a whole box of snack cakes—twelve servings if you can believe the label. My body squeals and groans, but my arms and legs have stopped flailing. It's like the new drugs are straps binding Madeline. They've got her wrapped up tighter than tight. I hear the straps straining, creaking. Someday they'll snap. They can't keep her tied up forever.

seventy-eight

i woke in the dark, in my pitch-black room, with someone holding my hand. A voice was crying, whispering softly, "Come back to me, Ellie. Please come back." My heart swelled. I thought it was Madeline until something hard and smooth grazed my knuckle—my mother's wedding ring. I pulled away and then regretted it. How could I be so mean? To my mother? She held my hand the entire time I was in the hospital. She was my only connection to this world. Without her I might have died. I reached through the darkness, searching for her fingers. The floorboards creaked, the door hushed closed. Too late. That's me with my mother, typical Ellie: always too little, always too late.

seventy-nine

the sign on Erika's door said BACK IN 5 MINUTES. I wanted to leave but I had nowhere to go. My mother wouldn't be back for an hour. I could sit in the reception area with the sickly lights and the fake plants and wait for Erika, or I could sit outside in the gray and the cold and wait for my mother. I stayed because it was my last session. The insurance company will pay for all the pills I'm on, but they won't pay for me to sit in Erika's office three times a week and talk about my problems. It's obviously a waste of my time and their money.

"Ellie, I'm sorry you had to wait," Erika said. "Come on in."

There was a can of chocolate diet shake on her desk and a plastic baggie with carrot sticks. Erika's nose was red—she either had a cold or she'd been crying. The hand sanitizer by her computer made me think it was a cold. She motioned toward the chair—my chair—and asked me to have a seat. She had her pad ready to take notes. I don't know why. After today, I'm not her responsibility.

"How are the new meds working for you?"

"Okay."

"School?"

"Okay."

"How are things going with your mom?"

"Okay."

Today she wanted me to leave with a blueprint for creating change. She gave me some paper to write stuff down because I didn't have my journal with me. It was my last day. I didn't think I'd need it. While Erika blew her nose, I wrote down *blueprint* and underlined it. I wrote down *change*, too.

"Life is full of choices, Ellie. There's always a choice. Some choices are healthy and some choices are unhealthy. In our last session, you expressed some concern about weight gain and grades."

I knew where she was going. My grades suck. I'm getting fat again. Worse than fat. Bloated. I look like I've been sucking on a bicycle pump.

"Do you think you've been making healthy choices?"

What choices do I really have? Name one. I didn't choose any of this any more than I chose to be born. My life was a train wreck before my body ever saw the light of day. I wanted to say something snotty—it's not like I'll ever see her again—but I couldn't. "No," I said. "I've been making really bad choices. I've been watching a lot of TV instead of studying. I've been eating a lot of junk."

"That's good, Ellie," she said. "Not your choices, but accepting responsibility for them."

I swallowed funny and started coughing. When I caught my

breath, she said she wanted us to make a list of positive choices, life-changing choices. She made me write them down. I don't remember them all, but mainly it was crap like:

I can choose to set goals for myself.

I can choose to forgive my mother.

I can choose to let people into my life and make new friends.

I can choose to accept my illness and choose to get well and choose to let Madeline go.

As I wrote, I thought, *I can choose not to sit here and listen to your crap about how my messed-up life is all my fault.*

"My mom's picking me up early," I said. "I have to go."

"Wait," Erika said. "I have something for you." She went to her desk and pulled out a drawer and handed me a copy of the phoenix poster, a smaller version of the one hanging on her wall. My parting gift. I walked out of her office and into the first bathroom and tossed my notes in the trash. The poster, I kept. The poster is cool.

eighty

It's not like being dead. I know what that's like, and this isn't it. Being dead is a lot like dreaming, but this isn't a dream. This isn't even a nightmare. This is nothing. They're poisoning me. I am empty inside, like some creepy jack-o'-lantern. And now I'm starting to rot.

I have choices. Erika said so.

I smile at my mother and put the pills on my tongue.

Upstairs, I spit the pills in the toilet.

eighty-one

it's been ten days since I stopped taking my pills. The hum is back. The humming in my head that means I'm alive. I feel like I'm on another kind of drug, a good drug, a white-hot star burning through the fog. I can think again. I can feel. For the first time in a long time I'm comfortable in my skin. It's the dead of winter, but everything sparkles and blooms. Everything is so intense, so alive. It's like waking up from one of those dreams where you think you're already awake—you're in your bed, in your room, and your room is your room exactly—but you're paralyzed. You try to lift your arm, but it feels like lead. Your lips are sewn shut. People are standing over you, talking and staring, but you can't move, you can't respond. Now that I'm awake, really awake and not dreaming, not paralyzed, I can't stop moving. I never want to sleep again. I want to be doing something every minute. I want to run through the woods. I want to smoke cigarettes with Autumn behind her chicken coop. I want to twirl around the house and cut my hair and sing and write poems. I want to call up Rad and Jess and Kylie, and say, *Look, guys! It's me! I'm back!* It's torture at night, sitting in front of the TV with Mom, with Thing in my lap. My mother has noticed. She says I seem different, better. She thinks it's the drugs working. She does not know. She says I'm more like my old self. *Which self, Mom?* There are so many Ellies, I can't keep track. I have to do something, anything, to keep from exploding, so I settle for homework and laundry and feeding the cat. I have to remind myself that it's all about killing time. I can't get too involved with other people. This is about my sister. I went off my drugs for her. She'll be back. I know it. I keep rereading our conversations in my old journal—the one with the Pegasus on it. There's a plan. She had a plan. I have to be patient.

eighty-two

It's been twelve days, but she hasn't shown herself to me. Not yet. Every noise, every flicker, every draft makes my heart beat wildly. Usually it's just Thing, scampering from room to room, or the furnace kicking on, or the house groaning, shrinking in this bitter cold. In the dark, every shadow looks like Madeline. I stand frozen, my eyes straining, thinking she's taking shape in that corner, behind this door, at the top of the stairs. It's always the stupidest things that catch me off guard: the floor lamp by the computer, the sheets lumped beneath my comforter, my mother's robe hanging from the back of the bathroom door.

It's some drawn-out game of hide-and-seek. She's here. I know it. My mother confirmed it. Tonight after dinner, while we were doing dishes, she said, "I don't want Sweet Pea in the babies' room. That's why I keep the door closed."

I tossed some forks in the silverware drawer and said, "Yeah? So?"

"Then why do you keep opening it?"

"I'm not. I haven't."

My mother frowned at something stuck at the bottom of a pot. "I don't care if you go in there. Just keep the door closed."

Later, after my mother went to bed, I went upstairs to use the bathroom. I haven't been in my old room in weeks, not since I helped set up the bassinets. My mother's door was closed, but the hall was bathed in a cold, pale light. The door to the babies' room was open. With the tree gone, there's nothing to block the moon. The window glowed a ghostly white. The curtains are in the wash, and the rug is in the attic, so it's just the two basketlike beds with half-dome hoods.

I whispered my sister's name. The floorboards creaked. I took a step and froze. Something was scratching in the closet. It sounded like our stupid cat. She must have been hiding when my mother shut the door. But then the sound shifted and grew. No, not Thing. Something bigger. Something flapping. The sound of wings beating. I prayed it wasn't a bat. I shielded my face and cracked the door, waiting for it to swoop out. Nothing. I reached up and pulled the string. The light blazed. It was a bird. Not a real bird, though. A mythical one. The bare bulb shone on a girl in a field, a massive flaming creature rising up before her. It was the phoenix poster, the one Erika had given me, taped to the back wall.

eighty-three

Why can't everyone stop talking about the future? Autumn's been on a we-are-moving-to-the-city-after-we-graduate kick. She ordered some free maps and guides off the Internet, and now she's plotting our escape in three years. But I can't think that far ahead. At school, all anyone can talk about is the spring formal and the tryouts for some stupid musical that's a month away. My mother's just as bad. With her, it's all about the babies. Furniture for the babies, clothes for the babies, and a thousand other things we need to get ready before they're born. She toddles around the house preparing. Tomorrow means nothing to me. It's a black hole. I'm in a holding pattern. All I can think about is Madeline and my damaged brain. What if everyone was right? What if all this really is just a chemical imbalance? My brain tripping for the last six months? The drugs put everything right, leveled it all out, and now I'm left with nothing but myself. Maybe I hung that poster in the back of the closet just like I supposedly sent that e-mail to Priscilla and sent myself that death threat and drew that picture of the baby on the bathroom wall and sliced my own hand and wrote all that stuff in my old journal. If I believe that, then what do I do with my mother's reaction to the picture on the camera, with Autumn saying it was me who beat her up but it wasn't, not really? I'm sick or I'm haunted. It can't be both. There are things in this world that can't be explained. Ordinary people encounter the strange and incredible every day: UFOs, premonitions, telekinesis, Bigfoot, God. Why not me? I didn't think I'd miss Erika, but I do. She was someone to talk to, even if she was paid to listen.

I think Madeline is punishing me. She's angry because I ruined the plan. I didn't trust her. She wanted us to be together forever and I rejected her. She forgave me the first time, when I abandoned her in the In-Between, returning to my body, giving up her world for this one. I should've stayed dead. I know now that there's nothing to fear. To lose this body wouldn't be so bad. It's scarred and broken, used up. Why am I so afraid to give up this shell? She either hates me and wants me to suffer, or she's gone. For good. Dead like my father, never to return. The drugs killed her. She was poisoned. Maybe what I'm feeling—all this energy in my chest—is something else. Maybe my body is my body again.

eighty-four

It's not your body. It never was.

eighty-five

i am the monster. Me. Elanor, I guess. I don't know who I am anymore. It's like that picture of a chalice, the one where if you shift your focus it becomes two faces. She carved into my chest, scratched into the ultrasound, but I was too blind to see. Not Madeline and Elanor . . . ME. Her. Fourteen years ago . . . two souls . . . one body. This body belongs to her. I am the possessor. I don't deserve to be here. I have no right. I took what did not belong to me, stole my sister's life. I took what wasn't mine and ruined it the way Priscilla used to destroy the clothes she borrowed. That day when my mother pointed to the white bean in the ultrasound and said, "That's you" . . . she was wrong. I was the void on the right, the one that shrank to a pinprick. I was the twin who vanished. My sister drew me into her, tried to save me, and I pushed her out. I'm a parasite. Worse than a parasite. I can live without her . . . but this isn't living.

eighty-six

The nervous energy is back, the grinding in my head. I can't sleep. Today I skipped lunch and went to the drugstore and bought more pills and hid them in my bag. I bought a box of matches, too. I don't know why.

eighty-seven

My mother knows that what happened today is not possible. I'm not superhuman. She'll try to explain it away, like the picture on the camera, but she can't. The furniture didn't move itself. Tomorrow she'll say I'm stronger than I look. She'll say I got help. Someone came over while she was out. *The joke's over,* she'll say. *You can just call up Autumn, or whoever, and tell them your mother said you need to put everything back.*

But I can't undo it because it wasn't me. Earlier I'd taken a pill to stop the grinding in my head. I was asleep on the couch. It was dark and the TV was blaring and my mother had gone to town for milk and gas because a storm is coming. She wasn't gone long—forty minutes, maybe an hour. There wasn't time. She knows that. Through the fog of pills, I heard her come home. She stomped her boots, put the groceries away, and climbed the stairs. I heard her in the hall. I heard her call my name and shout about the door being open again. Before I could say I didn't do it, my mother was coming back down, shouting about "last straws."

"You think that's funny? You're trying to be funny?"

I forced my eyes open. My mother was standing over me, her face purple with rage, her hands gripping the sides of her belly like it was a ball she was about to pass.

"What are you talking about?"

"Don't play stupid with me," she said, dragging me off the couch and up the stairs, her razor-sharp nails digging into my skin.

I tried to pull away. "Get off me!" I screamed. "I didn't do anything!"

When she showed me—shoved me through the door and into the room—I felt sick to my stomach. My legs went weak. It was the same cold tingling on the back of my neck that I used to feel when Scilla and I stayed too late in the cemetery and had to run past the crypts in the dark. All the heat left my hands and feet. Cold air was coming from somewhere. My mother was losing it, touching my things and crying: "What is this about, Ellie? Talk to me. Please just talk to me." But I couldn't because I can't tell her what I know. I can't tell her that her daughter, my sister—the one who should be living this life—wants what is hers. I can't tell her that I'm not supposed to be here, that this body is not my body. I stole it.

I'm sleeping downstairs tonight, on the couch. All the lights are on. My mother's freaked out, too, but she won't admit it. She unscrewed the hook-and-eye latch on the basement door and put it on the door to the babies' room. She said it's to keep the cat out, but I'm not stupid. The cat won't go near the babies' room, which is my room again until we get everything moved back downstairs.

The paneled room off the hall off the kitchen is empty. Everything I own is back in the Nacho-Cheese-and-Chips room—my bed, my desk, my dresser. It looks exactly like it used to except for the bassinets. They're still in there, pushed up against the wall, under the window. The message is clear: *That's* her *room*.

eighty-eight

W e're in the middle of a blizzard. We're stuck in this house, hemmed in by drifts. Snow hisses against the windows, churns hypnotic spirals in the sky. The front yard looked pure and clean and white until the guy across the road plowed. Now the driveway looks like an open grave. I don't know why he bothered. There's nowhere to go. Listen to the radio: the roads are closed, schools are closed. Even the mail was three hours late. The snow is erasing everything. The mountains, the woods behind our house, the houses on our road. All of it's gone, buried beneath a dull white blanket that melts into a dull white sky. It's deafening, the quiet. Only death and destruction rip through the muffled silence—gunfire, a baby shrieking.

Babies dying. Elanor's crying. Concentrate. Concentrate.

The gunfire is tree branches snapping under all that weight. The baby? My mother thinks it was a rabbit. We heard the dogs last night, howling, calling, and then the screaming, choked and desperate.

My mother thinks it's peaceful. She's enjoying this surprise break from school and studying. She waddles around the house with a dust rag and a can of lemon polish, cleaning, organizing, making everything perfect. She's nesting, she says. All pregnant women do it. It's another one of those weird urges they get. We've talked about The Day. It's not far off, only a few months. Everything's moving so fast. Next month my mother takes the test to get her real estate license. We've talked about that, too, how she's planning to go to work for the woman who sold us this house. We've talked about the summer, and how I can watch the babies while she's off showing properties. We've talked about next fall, and how she's going to have to find a good babysitter—maybe Autumn's grandma can do it, or else she'll have to put an ad in the paper.

What we haven't talked about is the room. We haven't talked about the latch on the door. We haven't talked about how the couch has become my bed or how I'm going through all our batteries sleeping with the flashlight shining on my face. We pretend everything is normal, like there's nothing strange about the way Thing startles for no reason, puffing her tail and arching her back.

Maybe it doesn't matter. The snow is swallowing everything. Maybe I won't have to make a decision, which is good, I guess, because I don't know what to do. I feel like my life is some twisted game show. Curtain number one is a lifetime supply of drugs. Curtain number two . . . a shiny new blade with my name on it.

eighty-nine

i felt her before I saw her. Felt her weight on the end of the couch. I aimed the light at my feet. Madeline was standing on the arm, her arms spread wide for balance, her skin so bright it hurt my eyes. She'd been adding to the feathers. She's covered in ink. My stone angel. Wings black as coal. *I'm here for you,* she said, and my fears dissolved. She's not evil or mean or vindictive. She had to do the things she did so I wouldn't get too attached to this life. There's a plan. I have to trust her. I was flooded with warmth and calm and something deeper than happiness. Peace. Something absolute and without end. The same feeling I used to get when my father would take me out to that field to watch the stars moving through the night sky. Her eyes burned, threaded with flames. I knew that look, the feeling behind it. The feeling of wanting to be wanted.

We didn't speak. We didn't have to. Madeline crawled toward

me, along the length of the couch, then slipped into the space between my body and the cushions, folding me in her arms. Her breath on my cheek had the electric smell of a storm coming. The flashlight on her face illuminated the ugly little scars identical to mine. I thought of her wrists and those perfect white strokes. Every pain I'd ever inflicted on myself I'd inflicted on her, too. I could hear my own heart, a sickly hollow thumping sound. This body has too much history. Madeline kissed my tears (her tears) pooling along the bridge of my nose (her nose). She stroked my ear (her ear), smoothed my hair (her hair).

She pulled the comforter over our heads and switched off the light. Side by side, safe and warm in the dark and in the silence, I remembered what it was like in the beginning, before my body vanished, before the two became one, and the one was just me, alone and lost, searching for what could never be again. We want the same thing, to end this aching loneliness, this always longing to be whole.

I've missed you. I love you.

I love you, too.

I'm sorry. I know what I've done. I never want to lose you again.

You won't.

I want to be with you always, but I'm afraid to die.

Who said anything about dying? It's not too late. There's time. The stars are waiting.

ninety

You think you know how this ends. You think it ends in the closet, with my old wounds reopened, The Last Song playing. You think it ends in blood, but it doesn't. It ends in flames. No body. No bones. Just a pile of ash. Some things can't be explained, like the bond between twins. I'm here to tell you there are no endings, only beginnings.

Today I said good-bye—silently, in my heart—to Rad and Jess and Kylie, to my teachers and Coach Buffman and Ms. Merrill. I wish I could tell them it's not their fault, no one's to blame. All of this was meant to be. I thought about sending something to Scilla, but that was a past life. Soon this will be a past life, too. The plan is the same. My mother was pregnant when I died—our bodies were pinpricks of light, distant stars—but then I didn't die, and everything got so complicated. It would've been easier if I'd resisted the tug of this world when I had one foot in the grave. Easier for everyone. For Autumn. For my mother. She's the one I'm worried about. Autumn will understand—eventually. She will believe. I've told her everything—about Madeline and the body that's not mine and the cycle as my sister explained it. I showed her the feathers—I'm covered in feathers now, too. Last night, Madeline finished my back. I showed Autumn as proof. I told her everything. Almost. I didn't tell her about the clubhouse, how Madeline's been working every night, building a nest of twigs and sticks, and how it's ready.

I used to think I didn't belong in this world. But I do, just not here, not now, not in this body. It wasn't mine to begin with. This life I borrowed—stole—was a disaster. I'm not deluding myself. My new life won't be perfect. I am who I am—that won't change. It'll still be me but in a different body—my own body—but this time I won't have to go through life alone. It's not like this for everyone. Everyone doesn't get a second chance. My father didn't.

I would be lying if I said I wasn't afraid. I took some extra pills and now my eyelids are heavy, my heart is slow and sure. The girls are outside—the girls that are our future—standing in the driveway, staring up at my window. They're wearing identical dresses, like they're going to a party. But it's midnight and cold, the kind that rips the air from your lungs, and they're not wearing coats. They'll be warm soon. Madeline strikes a match. Her breath smells like gasoline. If I can get to the nest and go to sleep, Madeline will take care of the rest.

Autumn will smell the smoke first—the sharp tang of burning wood. She'll look out her window and see a flickering, and then flames rising—higher and higher—scorching the bare branches. The woods behind her house will glow bright as dawn. No one will try to stop the fire. It's too far back, far enough from the house and the barn. They'll let it burn down to ash. My mother will come in to wake me tomorrow, to tell me about Autumn's clubhouse, but my bed will be empty. She'll sit at my desk and pick up this journal and read what I have written. She will check the closet anyway, wonder at the poster taped to the back wall, then wander the house calling my name. When I do not answer, she'll run stumbling through the snow through the woods to the still-smoldering clubhouse and drop to her knees like she's been shot. She will rock back and forth, clutching her belly, and scream. She will feel like the world is ending, collapsing. She will feel her heart kick and think she's dying.

And then she will feel me kick inside her.

She'll want to believe but can she? In the end, it's all about believing.

Before I understood everything, before my dawning, Madeline asked me what I wanted most in this world. I knew the answer then and it is the same answer today. It will be the same answer always. I want to be whole. I want to be loved. Everything is temporary—happiness, pain, grief, sadness—everything except this longing.

We have to go now.

I'm ready. It's a moonless night, but Madeline will be my eyes. She will guide me—my stone angel—through the dark woods and into the light.

ninety-one

i'm still here.

I should feel like one of those people who decide at the last minute not to get on a plane that ends up crashing. Lucky. But I don't feel lucky. Maybe someday. Not now. It's too soon to tell if I made the right decision. Everything happened so fast, there was no time to think. My mother was calling. Madeline was calling. I had to choose and I chose my mother. She needed me. She was bleeding. Not a lot, but enough to scare me. I thought she was dying. But it wasn't her blood. It was my blood. Not from this body, but the other one. Because I'm still here.

Madeline is gone. The clubhouse is in ashes. I have to believe I belong here, in this world. Right here. Right now. I hope so. There's no going back.

ninety-two

My mother is hooked up to machines that monitor the baby, the one that survived—Madeline. I'm with them now, in the chair beside the bed, listening to my sister's heartbeat. She's no longer a ghost, a lost soul. She's flesh and blood and bone. Losing her is hard. Because I have lost her, in a way. Things will be different now. The bond has been broken. My sister is still my sister, but she's not my twin. We will never be that close again. Everything we share is gone: our history, our dreams, our scars. There's so much she'll never know, never understand, about me, about us. I'll be the big sister, with my own life, separate from hers. It'll be me watching over her instead of the other way around. I can't fail her, not again. I can't fail my mother, either. I'm trying to be a good daughter. I bring her milkshakes from the cafeteria, magazines from the gift shop. This morning, before Autumn's mom drove me to the hospital, I cleaned up all the blood.

A nurse comes in and lifts my mother's hospital gown, exposing her hard, taut belly. The skin ripples like the surface of a pond. My mother lets me touch her. I feel an arm, a leg. My sister is reaching for me. I'm supposed to be in there with her. Not in some medical-waste bin, waiting to get tossed in an incinerator with amputated limbs and diseased organs and other lost babies. Reduced to ashes like my father. We're alike in so many ways. I'll probably spend the rest of my life fighting the darkness I inherited from him. But I've got my mother in me, too. She lives in the light. For me it is an endless cycle of light and dark. Right now everything is gray. The birds on the window ledge, the dying light in this room, the hair at my mother's temples.

The nurse leaves and my mother closes her eyes. I watch her belly rise and fall, and my ears fill with a sound like water rushing down a storm drain.

ninety-three

My mother is home, asleep in her bed. I'm in my bed, too. But I'm not alone.

"What are you writing?"

"Nothing."

"Can I read it?"

"No."

Autumn shrugs, scratches Thing behind the ears, and goes back to her plans. The clubhouse is gone, but she wants to rebuild. This summer, she said, when her brother is home on leave. Something bigger and better and sturdier. I hope she picks a different spot. The surrounding trees are scorched black, the bark blistered, permanently scarred, like me. The cuts on my face are nearly gone, but the others will be with me forever. My wrists remind me of what I almost gave up: my life. The ones over my heart, who I am: ME. EM when I look in the mirror. Elanor

Moss. Not Old Ellie or New Ellie or Madeline's Sister. I'm broken but whole, like my mother's favorite lamp. There's a fine crack down the center but it still works. That story about the gods splitting us in two—maybe it's not what it seems. Maybe your other perfect half isn't roaming the earth. Maybe your other perfect half is closer than you think. It would be just like the gods to send us in the wrong direction, dooming us to an eternity of searching for ourselves in others, looking outside when we should be looking in. Stupid, right? Maybe. Maybe not. I've been thinking about that a lot lately.

I've been thinking about Autumn, too. She is my friend. My one and only friend. She's not Madeline, but Madeline isn't Madeline anymore. My mother's naming the baby Francine, after my father's mother. My mother was right. We're a lot alike—Autumn and me. More than I want to admit. That's not how it sounds. It's just that it's hard sometimes, looking at your own reflection. Rad and Jess and Kylie—they weren't ever anything to me. And Scilla . . . was she ever really my friend? Yes. When we were little, but then we grew up, and she changed and I changed. And maybe someday Autumn will change, too. But right now we have each other. That means something, right?

Tomorrow, after school, I'm buying a new journal. I'm tired of this one. I don't care if it's only half full. So I guess that's it for now. I have to work on my endings.